VELVET DARK

A New Zealand Noir Tale

Brent Partner

Orlac Press

Auckland, New Zealand

Copyright © 2017 by **Brent Partner**

All rights reserved. No part of this publication may be reproduced, distributed or transmitted in any form or by any means, without prior written permission.

**Brent Partner/Orlac Press
Casuarina Road
Auckland, New Zealand, 2012**
http://brentpartner.com

Publisher's Note: This is a work of fiction. Names, characters, places, and incidents are a product of the author's imagination. Locales and public names are sometimes used for atmospheric purposes. Any resemblance to actual people, living or dead, or to businesses, companies, events, institutions, or locales is completely coincidental.

Book Layout © 2017 BookDesignTemplates.com
Book Cover Design: Y. Nikolova at Ammonia Book Covers
ISBN-13: 978-1719223195
ISBN-10: 171922319X

Velvet Dark/ Brent Partner. -- 1st ed.

To Eva and Jacob

For a Tear is an intellectual thing,
And a Sigh is the sword of an Angel King,
And the bitter groan of the Martyr's woe
Is an arrow from the Almighty's bow.

—WILLIAM BLAKE

Contents

1. 1
2. 5
3. 17
4. 29
5. 31
6. 51
7. 69
8. 83
9. 97
10. 115
11. 133
12. 149
13. 151
14. 169
15. 185
16. 199

17. 211

18. 213

19. 215

20. 229

21. 245

22. 247

23. 263

24. 277

25. 291

1.

'I spy with my little eye -'

'Please Dom, that's enough son. We've been doing this for hours.' I looked over at him in the back seat. His eyes sparkled like tiny jewels in the morning light. 'Just give Dad a few minutes -'

'He's only playing,' Jo snapped. 'A boy's entitled to a little fun - isn't he?'

I closed my eyes momentarily to the sprawl of Mt Albert traffic. 'Don't start, love. I'm tired and I've got to meet him this afternoon.'

'Keep your eyes on the road. We're all dead tired. All of us,' Jo said. 'Where?'

'Some café on K Road. I wonder if it's the same...'

'Well I don't want to see him and I don't want Dominic anywhere near him. You can drop me off at Mums.'

'Who are you going to see, Dad?' Dom piped in. I never wanted to name him Dominic – kids called Dominic got bullied.

'Just someone I used to know, son. Don't worry about it.'

'Just you see that you do worry about it,' Jo said. 'I want this over done with - once and for all.'

'That's what we're here for, isn't it? Bit of a waste of time otherwise. He says he needs someone who knows about cars.'

'I don't want to know, Bill. Get it done.'

'Christ's sake, Jo. Stop going on about it – I told you didn't I?'

'I spy with my little eye...'

My eyes were closed again as we crossed from Mt Albert into Sandringham.

***

We turned into a secluded avenue. I hadn't seen this street in years but it still tasted of condescension and felt like inadequacy. I parked outside the dull blue villa with its manicured verges and trimmed hedges. There was no car in the driveway. No signs of life.

'Doesn't look like anyone's home. Do you want me to wait around for a bit?'

'I know where she keeps the key. No need to stick around,' Jo said, 'I know you don't want to.'

'Right then,' I said. 'I'll call you when I'm settled in.'

She avoided my kiss. Just opened the door and got out. 'Get it done quickly, Bill. We won't wait forever.'

I closed my eyes. 'See you later.'

Opening them again I saw them in the driveway. Dom was crouching, examining something on the ground. Jo was turned away from me – that seemed to be the scheme of things these days. How did they get there so fast?

Time was a funny thing.

2.

Karangahape Road seemed like a woman's spine. It lay recumbent, sloping away from the lush harbour towards the tawdrier Kingsland. Pitt Street marked the small of the back; Upper Queen Street, the place where the breasts might drop; a sultry invitation to Newton Gully to find some comfort there. K Road was a nightclub singer of a street and her age was a study in evolution. The early hours of the evening saw her as nubile, unblemished and filled with hope, but as evening wore on she aged, tired from singing too long to people in the same old dive. The death of night marked her barren and lifeless. Waiting for the end as the dawn appeared over the Southern motorway.

I sat on a marble bench, shaped it seemed in honour of the surrealists. That was a difference between then and now – my arse forever noticed what it sat on now, ever conscious of the threat of haemorrhoids. But everyone got older – if not wiser.

The cavalcade of vehicles crept, slow and impatient. Occasionally a brief stutter of movement sped up the train of steel and rubber from its dawdling progress. But these were only passing moments. A respite like a desperate breath. Soon it would be stifled by the traffic lights of the Queen Street intersection. Inactivity fuelled the slow build-up of exhaust fumes and mingled with coffee bean, incense and commuter sweat.

I stared along the old madam to see what was different.

On a visual level - the cut of the facades, the sight of the pedestrians – everything seemed familiar. Sure, businesses had gone to be replaced by newer ones. But that had always been the way. Capitalistic sensibility have never really held sway here. Art and culture had always been the dominant flavour over the clank of the cash register. So the businesses, like the flower, sprouted and radiated unto their zenith – then gradually faded. Withered in the autumn of their short lives and disappeared into obscurity. But with the cycle of the seasons, new blooms erupted to replace the fallen ones. Fresh colour marked K Road as a place forever in transition. It was metamorphosis in practice.

I glanced at my watch with its battered leather strap that threatened to split and fall away. I would have to meet him soon at the Odyssey.

The café had not been here twenty years ago. It was in the hands of the gods whether it would be here in the new millennium, a little less than a month away. If it had been here back in the day, I doubt I would have even made it through the doors. The young punk that I was would never have been seen dead in there anyway. I had never been part of any art crowd.

My concentration was broken by two well-used plastic shopping bags that passed into view at my feet. A ragged man approached. His dreadlocks were matted and filthy and they twisted away below his waist. They surrounded a brown face, marked by the harsh excesses of a hard life.

'Gotta cigarette, brother?' he said.

I reached into the inside pocket of my out-of-date jacket and shook one from a packet. Hobo hands – liberally inked with cobweb tattoos – snatched at it.

'God bless you brother...I'm a man of the streets you know.'

'Really? I would never have guessed.' My dry wit evaporated and lost itself amid the exhaust fumes.

'How 'bout two bucks.'

'Fuck off now. I've got things to do.'

'C'mon brother, you can afford it.' His rasp had turned into a higher toned wheedle. I did not reply.

Instead I turned away and he drifted past.

'You sly bastard, I saw you.' Another of the homeless, female and equally ragged, slipped out of a shop front and confronted her comrade.

'What?'

'I saw it, you scabby ole prick.'

The conflict between the two intensified; the animosity of it all hit me across the distance.

'I'm a king of the streets.'

'You're a dirty, smelly bastard.'

'Good looking one though. I'm a ladies man.'

'I'll get laid quicker than you.'

'Bitch.'

'Arsehole.'

The vitriolic cycle seemed doomed to continue, building with the imminent danger of a thunderstorm. I had started this at a small cost. The thought amused me then brought me down with the futility of it all.

Looking back at the ground, I sighed, fumbled in my pockets and drew out a cigarette. I lit it and blew oil-blue smoke out onto the street. What the fuck was I doing here? Everything was different. Nothing was quite the same.

'Jesus, Myers. You look like shit.' The voice was raspier but still familiar sounding. It came from behind me. I didn't have to guess who it was.

Steerforth was a fat man now. His shaved head was stubbled in grey. Back in the day, his looks were his godhead. Women stuck to him like flies to shit. Not so now. He had jowls for cheekbones, two chins instead of one and a myriad of vein and artery were splayed liberally under the eyes.

Still came across like style. The black silk of a designer shirt helped conceal the swollen midriff, a large diamond stud was buttoned in an ear, fat red crepe-soled shoes below moleskin trousers and he still had that look. Arrogance blended with the innocence of a child. It washed away all the initial feelings of dislike.

'You don't look like shit,' I said, 'you look like bloated shit.'

Steerforth didn't reply. He merely looked back at me devoid of all emotion. My gut clenched with uncertainty, then released, as Steerforth laughed from deep inside his belly. He trapped me in a hug that smelt of Old Spice and nicotine.

'Touché,' he said, 'I'd forgotten your razor wit. But if it were me, I would have just called me a fat cunt and be done with it. How long's it been?'

'I don't know,' I lied, 'Fifteen years or so, give or take a few months.'

'And nothing from you till yesterday?'

'Well there was Jo.'

'Ah Jo, how is she?'

I felt my cheeks redden. 'Alright I guess. I still see her now and again.'

'Really? I would have cut all strings from her. Onwards and upwards, Bill,' he said. 'Let's get inside. These vagrants make my skin crawl.'

It was good not to hear empathy. It made things easier. That was enough. That was more than enough.

I wondered if he knew what Jo had made of herself. Steerforth knew the eighteen year old girl he had dumped. But what about the woman, the complicated adult she had become? Steerforth had the comfort of forgetting her. I had not. For me there was never any forgetting.

We made our way past the homeless combatants of the ensuing battle. Mr Dreadlocks, as I now thought of him, looked up. His expression opened with confusion, recognition and finally the sort of businesslike calculation one finds with the poor and the desperate. It was like viewing a set of time-lapse stills in quick progression. Too fast to be static – too slow to display fluid motion.

'Hey Steery, remember me?'

Steerforth looked right through the tramp. I could smell the distaste; it was sour with disdain.

'Do I know you?' he said.

'I know you, Steery. Give us two bucks.'

'What?' Steerforth said, 'Why don't you get a job like normal people? Get the hell away from me.' With that, he shoved the bum away. The force was too great for his legs and he sat down hard.

Grabbing Steerforth by the elbow, I led him away. Mr Dreadlock's companion had vanished once more, seemingly melted into the doorways and shop-fronts.

'Get off him, Alan. C'mon, let's get that drink.'

Steerforth turned back on me with an easy smile. 'Drink – yeah. Don't call me Alan. I don't like it.'

'Whatever man, let's get in. I'm thirsty.'

We passed through the fashionably peeling doors into the interior. Inside, aubergine walls displayed a certain Forties chic with glimpses of deco. A row of trapezoid shaped lights shone an aqua glow onto a long bar front. It wasn't busy, but the hum of conversation felt amplified in the long narrow form of the room.

'Get us some drinks. I've gotta take a leak,' Steerforth said. 'Tell whoever to put it on the tab. Whiskey Sour for me.'

I wandered over to the bar; placed my shoe on the high foot rail and leaned forward and tried to catch an eye. The bartender was young but had a lot of experience burnt in his eyes. He carefully avoided my gaze, lips pursed in petulance at the very notion of my presence. What seems like a minute passed until my patience broke. 'Excuse me, pal,' I said.

His eyes squinted in the tradition of crappy bar staff everywhere. 'Can I help you?'

'Vodka & Tonic and a Whiskey Sour. On Steerforth's tab, if you please.'

The boy/man looked up and down the length of me with a look of contemptuousness that made me acutely aware of my out-of-date clothes, scuffed shoes and the three day growth on my cheeks. I brushed the sweat back through my hair. The need for a cigarette coursed through me.

'Steerforth's tab? You sure about that?'

'Positive. He's in there,' I said, pointing at the busy restroom door. 'He told me to get them in.'

With a sigh that seemed to have passed over his lips many times before, the bartender turned away. He returned with the order and set it down hard on the counter, slurps of mixer dripped over the rims. 'You sure you're with him? No free rides here.'

'I'm sure, pal.'

A booth lay spare in the corner that seemed to offer a modicum of privacy. The environment of Odyssey seemed alien to me. It belonged to a culture that had passed me by without my knowledge. I had never really been a member of any in-crowd, but at least then my youth camouflaged me to a degree. I noticed at the bar a couple: spiky-haired, with that heroin chic that I had always loved. They kissed with a brazenness that I forever wished I could have emulated in public.

'So why are you here, Bill?' Steerforth's voice came from behind me. Half his glass was emptied in one brave gulp before I answered.

'Told you on the phone. Reliving my past, finding what I missed out on when I left.'

'All that costs money, Bill. How are you going to live? This is an expensive town.'

'I've got money enough. Years with a handbrake will do that for you. I got money from the workshop when I sold it.'

'Shit, rent will suck you dry in months. I'll give you a job...what I told you on the phone.'

Trying not to appear too eager, I looked into my drink as if in some deeper form of contemplation. 'No offence,' I said, 'it doesn't sound entirely legal.'

'I'm legit – think about it. Place to stay, cash and the odd perk. New Year's Eve isn't far off. We're going to be run off our feet on New Year's Eve – it's a new century'

'I don't know. I wouldn't know what to do. Shit, I'm still married.'

'So are most of my customers. What are you – a choirboy or something?'

'No.'

'Well then, be the best driver I've ever had.'

Looking at him brought it all back. The spell of the man, the bluster, the smile that hid the contrast beneath. It was a face that was hard not to like.

'Well,' I said, 'I do know my way around a car...'

'Tell you what,' he said, 'we'll finish up here and you can follow me over. It's on Sandringham Road – not far away. Stay a few days and if you are comfortable, start driving for me. Can't say fairer than that.'

Game on. Steerforth the player. Just doing his old mate a favour. Old mate. What a fucking joke.

'Ok, I suppose,' I said.

'Good man. That's the Myers I knew.'

Later, drunk and a little obnoxious, we hit the newly formed winter night. K road had not yet hit middle age: the bloom of youth still dusted her asphalt cheeks.

As I gunned my beat up station wagon down the New North Road, following Steerforth's sleek BMW I realised what was different. It was me.

Before I was alive, now I only existed.

3.

I lifted the car door on its hinges, slammed it shut and walked the length of the gravel driveway alongside the building. Weeds sprouted in a jumbled fashion where the outer face of the wall met the rock floor. Where the tyres had not rutted the ground; wild patches of grass pointed back at their wall-bound companions.

The two-storey affair was old, weatherboards were cracked and the paint had long since peeled revealing previous tints indistinguishable in the twilight. The wooden slats however, displayed a patchier colour scheme. The aerosol art of a tagger flaunted a nom-de-plume halfway along the boards. It was part picture and part textual. A portion of both but not wholly either.

The disguised lettering held no meaning for me. Someone less puzzling had sprayed, *THUG,* in dribbling white upper case over the work. As I passed onto Sandringham Road however, the character of the building changed. A small-segmented block of shops with that sense of personality to it; from times when people had a closer relationship with commerce.

The frontage was licked with new paint: a dispassionate cream with a forest green trim. A small neon sign winked an azure, *Nymphs,* from the corner of a bay window.

I imagined, that once, this could have been a different place of convenience. Perhaps a pharmacy – where Edwardian women with choker collars and hip swelling corsets would have bought castor oil and mustard poultices for their bony sons and daughters. Or maybe there had always been a brothel here. Perhaps the same starched collars and uncomfortable boots that passed before a priestly rostrum every Sunday morning, journeyed through this particular doorway the previous Friday night.

Steerforth was waiting impatiently for me outside the door. Above a small plaque announced: *For the Discerning Gentleman.*

I felt the impending threat of laughter build up inside me. Vodka always found a funnier side of me. 'Never thought of you as discerning, mate.'

'Oh that's just there to make the joint sound classy – for the punter's benefit. Makes them think they're getting something for their money. What do you think?'

'It's a whorehouse, that's what I think. Bit out of the way too.'

A slight frown creased Steerforth's jowls, making them bounce slightly. 'We do mainly outwork but there are rooms too. People find us ok. And there's the bar you'll work in the quiet times.'

'I haven't decided yet.'

'What else are you going to do? Good digs upstairs as well. Not bad at all.'

He opened the door and we walked into a narrow foyer. The floor was a mosaic, a profile of a Romanesque woman in supplication. To the right, there was an ornate entrance. Straight ahead lay a plainer affair. Steerforth drew out a set of keys and unlocked the simpler option. 'Club's through there,' he said, nodding at the other entry. 'You'll probably use this door more. You can get through there from your place, upstairs.'

The open door revealed a steep and narrow cast stairwell. Textured walls complemented the stairs that flaunted dense shag pile carpeting.

'Onwards and upwards, Bill,' Steerforth said. 'Onwards and upwards.'

An apartment unfolded at the head of the stairs. Steerforth flicked on the light switch. It wasn't bad – not bad at all. It was minimal. Its only functional features – a queen size bed, couch, desk and a coffee table with a small television placed on top – all seemed to be located in exactly the right places.

The walls displayed carefully positioned art that reflected the overall tone of the room. This combined with the strategic halogen lighting, gave off the sentiment of a gallery. One of those places that I would have walked right past on Ponsonby Road because I wouldn't have felt like I belonged there.

'No kitchen or anything,' Steerforth said, 'but with no rent – I figure you can afford to eat somewhere else.'

'Never been able to boil an egg anyway.'

'So you're coming round to the idea then?'

'Didn't say that – just said I couldn't cook.' I gestured grandly around the room. 'I never figured you for a man of taste, Steerforth.'

'Nothing to do with me. One of the girls was studying interior design. Cost me an arm and a leg, but you've got to live well.'

Steerforth sat down, produced a plastic bag from his pocket and spilled its powdery contents on the table. From his wallet he drew out a credit card and chopped and sorted the pile into four concise lines. The technique of his actions showed an almost tradesman-like pride. 'Want some?' he said, 'Business partner scored it from Sydney. Flaky not rocky.'

'What do you mean partner? I thought you owned this place outright.'

'I do but I've got other interests. Got to spread yourself wide to be successful, Bill.'

'You got that covered.'

He rolled a twenty-dollar note and inhaled half the available lines in two big snorts. Sniffing and watery-eyed, he looked across and offered me the tube.

'I don't know mate,' I said. 'Been a while – don't know if it's me now.'

'Only one way to find out, my friend. Give it a go.'

Friend? The joke was eternal. Annoyed, I took the tube and drew up the offerings with equal gusto to Steerforth's effort. The burn was instant in my sinuses. 'Fuck me,' I said.

'Gets in doesn't it?'

The elation hit and I was both indestructible and deconstructed all in one. I looked around the room with my refreshed psyche and noticed an innocuous door, the same colour as the wall coverings. I guess that's why I didn't notice it.

'We get in from there?'

'I thought you'd never ask,' Steerforth said, 'Locks from the inside. So no uninvited guests will bother you.'

He pulled it open and looked to me expectantly. 'No one has an easier commute to work. What do ya think?'

'I think you have just invented the door.'

Steerforth's eyes narrowed momentarily but returned with a twinkle. 'Whatever,' he said. 'Let's head down. I'll introduce you around.'

'What about my gear? It's still in the car.'

'Can't see it being worth nicking. You putting this off or something?'

'It's a different world that's all.'

'Let's do it,' I said and walked on through.

On the other side the lighting was noticeably dimmer. The style that was there behind me had gone, banished to the space beyond two inches of plasterboard and pine.

Before me, on the adjacent wall, hung a frame that enclosed a veneer of black velvet. Brushed onto the fabric was a semi-naked woman: alluring and seductive. The varnished shades of her contours glowed vibrant against the ebony background.

'My velvet beauty,' Steerforth said. 'Gets me every time. Worth a penny these days too. Like all the other women here.' He let out a snort that sounded piggish.

I felt myself drawn into the painting. The dark and exotic pulse of it struck a chord in what was left of my heart. My eyes traced the curves of her torso, the gentle slopes of her breasts and lingered over the darkened areola.

'Nice tits, eh,' said Steerforth.

'Enchanting.'

'Always the romantic son-of-a- bitch, Bill. You're so good at it now that you're standing with me in a brothel instead of being tucked up in bed with your wife.'

'It was ok for years,' I sneered. 'Where's your happy family?'

'At the end of the hall, Bill. At the end of the hall.'

We moved on down the passage. I could hear the floorboards creak under the strata of the carpet. The building was old and rheumatic yet still strangely alive under my feet. From behind a doorway a soft moan floated, coupled with a rush of movement.

'See?' Steerforth said. 'People find us fine. I'm not a cynical prick, Bill.'

'You know your business better than me.'

'Damn straight, I do – haven't been hiding my head in the sand for years. I know where I'm going.'

Steerforth opened the door at the end of the hall without knocking and gestured me inside.

'Sam,' he said, 'this is my old mate, Bill. I told you about him.'

A bull of a man. From the crown of his shaven head to the ends of his wing tips, Sam was mass in action. Perhaps it was the cut of his expensive looking suit, but it appeared as if someone forgot to attach a neck when he was assembled. Instead there was a dollop of brown flesh that hung over the tailored shirt collar that was maybe chin or maybe shoulder.

The weight that hung from his frame grasped to reach the floor. The distribution wasn't all moving in a downwards direction, the bulk of muscle supported what fat there was and held it firm. This played out in the easy way in which he crossed the room, hand extended in an affable welcome. 'Gidday,' he said. 'Sam Ngata. You're smaller than I expected.' His voice did not match the baritone of his body. Instead it came out as a passable tenor.

'Thanks – I think.'

'What do you think of the place?' Sam asked.

'This is all I've seen but it looks ok.'

'You haven't seen the rooms yet? They're themed. We got them all – a western room, a dungeon, a hay barn...' he said. 'I'll show you next door. It's empty at the moment.'

We moved back down the hall to an opulent room. In the far corner sat a deep hot tub housed in a marble veneer. The walls were draped with blue silk hangings. Imprinted upon them was a series of gold fleur-de-lis. The circular bed that sat at the centre of the room had similar patterns on its coverings.

'This is the Antoinette Room,' Steerforth said. 'Sam came up with the title. Didn't you Sam?'

'What else could you call it? It's obvious.'

'The Fuck Room,' said Steerforth.

'You're all class, Alan,' says Sam.

'Don't call me that.'

The silence that followed was raw. It was one of those uncomfortable places where I just didn't like to be. Quiet, when you were by yourself was comforting. Like this though, it was painful. I had to say something. For my own sake.

'All this must have cost a packet,' I said.

'Always pays to have friends in high places, Bill' Steerforth said, 'or low ones.'

'Yeah.'

The conversation seemed to have rolled over and died a particularly nasty death. I looked at the pair and felt the pharmaceutical and vodka wash dissipate from my body. All that was left was a sort of detached lethargy and a dry throat.

'I'm tired,' I said. 'If you don't mind, I'll get my head down. It's been a long day – I'm knackered.'

'You haven't met everyone yet,' Steerforth whined.

'Tomorrow,' I replied, 'it was a long drive from Levin.'

'What if I set you up with a girl for an hour? On the house. Then see how you feel.'

'I just need to sleep.'

Steerforth seemed put out. He looked at me, his bottom lip pouting in disapproval.

I shook Sam's hand, muttered some pleasantries that was conducive to these situations and wandered back down the passage.

'I'll send someone over later,' Steerforth called, 'just in case.'

'Don't bother. Thanks anyway.'

In my new room I flopped on the bed, and stared at the ceiling. The texture of it carried me off. I dreamt of her, young and tousle haired, laughing along Queen Street. I saw her again, older, with a far off smile and then again, red-faced after twelve hours of labour. Jo changed. She had fire in her eyes.

***

A hesitant tap woke me at the door later on. I just rolled over and dreamt of her some more.

4.

'What do you think?'

She gave a cursive sniff. 'It's a man's room – very practical.'

'A woman designed it.'

'For a man...'

'Well I like it – I think.'

'You're not here to like anything. Keep your mind on what it is you're here for.'

'I am. I haven't thought of anything else.'

'Do you mean it...really mean it?' She walked by me on the couch. Her hair smelt of jasmine, with a hint of cinnamon.

'I've driven hundreds of kilometres to be here. Of course I mean it...I love you.'

She paced the length of the room, her scent gone, replaced by her annoyance. 'Who's the bitch on the wall? Does she make you hard like I do?'

'It's a fucking painting. I like it – that's all.'

She leant in close, brushed her lips against my ear and whispered, 'But you love me.'

'You know that...it's just a damned picture.'

'If you don't do this thing for me, I'll leave you flat.'

'I'll do it. Don't leave me...I couldn't face it.'

5.

It took moments before Sam answered his office door. He ushered me through and gestured to the only available chair. Leaning forward across the desk he looked me directly in the eyes. It seemed to me that space itself, folded between us. The only separation, the clear jelly skin of two corneas and the wells of the souls beyond.

There was only Sam and the chair.

'Do you really want to do this work?' Sam said.

'Sure.'

'I'm serious. Steerforth's been blowing your trumpet, but I want you to consider it carefully. It can be a shitty job – good money but it hardens you. You're the only line of defence out there. Do the job half-arsed then someone gets hurt and that costs the business. Get it?' He leant in closer, clasping his meaty fingers before him. The silk sleeves of his shirt shimmered and threatened to split along the seams.

I felt myself sink further back into the chair. If only I could have looked somewhere else, but the pull of Sam's irises forbade it. It scared me to feel trapped like this. I was being played like a game and beaten soundly. 'I'm not stupid,' I said. 'I've never done something like this before but I'm a quick study. Tell me what to do and if I'm no good fire me.'

Sam's eyes crinkled at the corners and he sat back. I felt the release of their grip. A scissor cut shearing the bands of contact. The man that sat before me now seemed smaller than just moments before. A boyish smile played across his lips. 'You'll be fine,' he said. 'You just have to keep it real. Steerforth thinks it's a game. He's got the lifestyle but he avoids the day to day stuff. It's not a business to him. It's his personal kingdom.'

'I'm not Steerforth.'

Sam laughed. A belly laugh that rippled the silk fabric of his shirt in concertina fashion. 'I don't think anyone is – thank Christ.'

The office was an office once more. The air circulated like it should have. The long mahogany desk was no longer a wall that I was tethered to. I no longer felt like the lamb awaiting the slaughter.

'So what do I have to do?' I said.

'Well, we've a client in St Heliers in an hour. I'll come this time and show you what goes down.'

He looked me up and down in more than a cursory way – Da Vinci appraising the smile of his Lisa – and gave a sniff. I felt aware of the out of style Levis and polo shirt that clung to me. 'Got a suit?' he asked. 'We're in the selling game – got to give the right impression.'

I thought of the black single-breasted offering lying with the rest of my wardrobe. 'Got something that might do,' I said.

'Anything has got to be better than that. Might pass on the farm but we're a classy outfit.'

***

I knew my suit would not do. It had fit me since I was twenty-two. I laid it straight upon my bed. The nylon strands actually shone through what was left of the wool. It hadn't been dry-cleaned in an eon and wrinkles sat at cross purposes with other wrinkles across the surface. As I pulled on the trousers and slipped on the jacket over the rayon shirt, I felt the mantle of my former life fall upon my shoulders. I remembered each ragged coffee stain, each drop of food and each carelessly spilt ash of the past. Looking down the front, I spotted on the lapel, a hole where a cigarette had won through. I should have burnt this thing with the other stuff. The thought that I hadn't annoyed me.

Sitting on the bed, I clasped my head into my hands. This is what it had come down to. I was the worst dressed pimp in town. If this was some hip seventies B-grade film, I would have had the clothes to wear and a ride better than an Eighties Toyota station wagon. But still, I was closer now than before. The idea cheered me somewhat.

I stood and the scent of the past left me. For now the present was seeing me clear. A loser no longer, I left my room and pushed my way back into the parlour's hallways.

Standing before my velvet princess, I kissed two fingers lightly and caressed her crimson counterparts with them. She would be my companion tonight, entwined together in a maiden voyage. The romantic vision stayed with me as I sailed down the row of doors. A slight moan that escaped from behind one door came to me as the call of a gull lightly dancing on a Pacific skyline, banking and wheeling in a gentle updraft. A winged shadow performing an aerial ballet on a palette of red-orange and disappearing blue.

As I entered the office once more however, the gull folded away and plummeted like a rock downwards. I stood once more in my own reality.

'Jesus,' Sam said, 'were you in a coma for the last twenty years? I've seen more fashionable bums than you. Where've you been?'

'Married in Levin.'

'It'll have to do. But you're coming out tomorrow and I'm going to dress you properly. We'll write it off as an expense. Christ, you need doing.'

The door opened behind me. The woman who passed through looked at us and flopped onto the velour couch. There was an air of contempt about her – something repellent. Although looking at her, she was anything but. Her hair was set in a bob cut – sloppily arranged – and housed a face that in another life would have been called angelic. Not a model's face, no angles and planes with that sense of severity that came with it. The image that came to my mind was cherubic. She had petulant lips, full at the bottom that formed a natural pout, a slightly crooked nose, that added to her looks rather than detracting. She was pure sexy – earthy beautiful.

Her blue-grey eyes negated it all. Deadness lived in them, devoid of any apparent empathy. Not a lost hope look, rather it was as if hope never had showed up there in the first place. I am sure I'd never seen her before, but the look she gave me made me think that I had done her wrong in the past. I actually felt like apologising to her – for nothing at all. Her attitude was perplexing.

'Jasmine,' Sam said, 'this is Bill the new guy.'

She did not reply only gave a disinterested nod and looked far away.

'He's coming out tonight,' Sam continued. 'You're going to be a back seat driver for a while.' He laughed at his own joke, slipping me a wink at the same time.

Jasmine crossed her legs as if in reply. I caught a white sheen glimpse of her panties. Conscious of the focus of my gaze, I carefully looked away. My old suit trousers felt a flicker of long lost life beneath them. She giggled. The expression on her face transformed. The boredom was replaced by mischievous humour – almost feral. Her lips pursed in a Victorian doll pout, but the rest of her look was primal. The contrast stirred me, exuding something illicit there for the taking. It seemed something to be savoured. I felt the colour mounting in my face.

'Sure you're up for it?' she said. 'You don't want to get too stressed.' The voice that emanated from her mouth was vulgar, at odds with the image before me. All the feelings that had built in me drained away in her tone. The facets that made her disturbing were reflected in the timbre of her melody.

I smiled back at her. 'I'm sure I'll be just fine.' I turned to Sam. 'Let's do it, shall we.'

Sam opened a desk drawer and tossed me a set of keys. 'We'll take the BMW. Your car's like your clothes.'

Jasmine giggled again.

Sam turned on her, his voice took a harder line. 'You got everything?' he said. 'We're going to St Heliers again. You are not going to fuck around on him this time are you? Any more complaints and you're out on your arse. No more chances. Understand?'

She squirmed into the couch, abruptly looking very young. I felt her discomfort. I felt mine.

'I thought I didn't have to do him anymore,' she said. 'He's creepy and he hurts...'

'He's asked for you, doesn't want anyone else. If you got a problem, fuck off now.' Sam seemed to loom over her like a bloat-filled shark coming in for the kill.

'I'll do it,' she whispered.

'You better,' said Sam. 'Let's go.'

**

The air outside created a suggestion of mist behind the building. A vaporous breath formed a wash of condensation over the BMW, parked next to my car. Sam fitted himself into the passenger seat, his belly spilling over his belt. Reaching forward, he opened the glove box and took out a map book. 'Most important tool of your trade,' he said. 'If you're lost, we're not making money and the client cancels. Everyone thinks they know Auckland, but it takes a job like this to recognise they don't. Keep it with you always.'

'Where to,' I said.

'Covenant Street. Regular job like this and the girl will know the way. She'll help direct you.' He looked to the back seat. 'Won't you, Jasmine?'

Jasmine didn't reply, just fumbled in her bag. Pulling out a cigarette, she lit it and blew a plume of smoke out her open window.

We pulled out onto Sandringham Road. 'You arrive at the address,' Sam continued, 'and leave the girl in the car, knock on the door and get the money. Straight hour is two hundred and eighty dollars. Check out that the client's alone – you get a feeling if a place isn't cool. This is a regular gig, so we know everything is safe -'

A sharp snort of derision came from the back seat followed by a blue cloud of smoke. Sam glared behind and continued. 'Always ask the girl if she's good with the gig. They are more attuned because it's their arse on the line. Always be polite. There are a lot of pricks in this game but their money's just as good.'

It was a pleasurable ride. The car glided on the road. I felt I could steer with my fingertips. As we shot from the bottom of Parnell Rise onto the waterfront, I imagined we were entering a new type of land. To the left, silhouettes of trees planted at a uniform distance answered the rhythmical blink of cats eyes, entrenched into the asphalt surface of the road. We had moved into suburbia without quite realising when it happened. The only sound within the car was the weighty breath of Sam and a sporadic nicotine intake from behind. I didn't even notice these sounds; the journey was my only concern. This was motion with purpose, a fixed destination and a course already plotted back home.

We moved through the bay areas into St Heliers. Sam directed me to Covenant Street and got me to stop just before. 'I'll get out here,' he said to me. 'I've told you what to do. Do the business and then pick me up.' He turned behind to Jasmine. 'Ring me when you're through. Don't fuck it up.'

Sam pushed himself out. We left him behind, a mountain of shadow and turned up a wide short driveway. I used the lit porch of the house to guide me in. Taking a breath, I got out and tramped to the front door. Before I had time to knock, it opened furtively. The man that stood behind it was startling in his ordinariness. Fawn corduroy pants were topped by a green patterned jersey. He was late thirties, with a hairline in a state of severe recession. This guy wouldn't look at me. It made me feel dominant – I was in control. He has a fine featured face, its bone structure brittle, beyond delicate. Across the brim of his cheekbones, bedraggled strands of coarse hair hung where the razor has missed. Within the clutch of his almost skeletal hand, a wad of twenty-dollar bills are held. I feel at ease.

'You alone tonight, mate?' I asked. The punter only nodded and still managed to avoid my look. 'It's two eighty,' I continued.

He pushed the notes into my hands. His touch was clammy. I pocketed them without counting. Had to get Jasmine now – this I knew. I was suddenly aware of what I was actually doing. I was a fucking pimp. A sticky wash of sweat formed on my forehead.

Jasmine saved me. Her door opened and she slinked outwards. A transformation had occurred in the back seat of the BMW. This was not the dour woman who wouldn't look at me. There was no disdain or negativity. This was sensuality cloaked in a short black dress. Her every step measured to display the sway of her hips. Goddamn, it worked.

'You ok with this?' I asked.

'I'll call when I'm done,' she purred. Even her voice was sultry. This woman was an actress. She should have been in film.

The door closed behind them leaving me alone in the night. Numb, I trudged back to the driver's seat.

'That's how it's done,' Sam said as he got back in. 'You're busier most of the time but you'll get it. Let's go for coffee.'

***

We did the drive in silence. I didn't see the need for anymore conversation – neither, it seemed, did Sam. He just looked out the passenger window at the passing houses and elevated apartment blocks of the waterfront landscape. I concentrated on the rhythm of the night traffic and drifted into a philosophical state.

It was strange. I saw my married life as a series of still images that were somewhat grainy and overexposed. The edges just inside the frame were irresolute, beyond visual comprehension.

They did not come to me in sequence – more like a spilt collection of snapshots dropped from a coffee table onto the floor of my memory. The images on the top were the more poignant instances, fragments of significance. The others lay overlapping one another: half memories that formed secondary layers.

Certain moments however, were not static. They were vivid Super8 memories. Unlike film images, they were tactile. I could actually reach back and feel their vitality. Like any editor worth their salt, I could cut these images up and experience tiny moments of significance. Such as waking up to Jo for the first time.

'What's your name?' I said.

'Steady on tiger,' she replied, 'just because you sleep with a girl, doesn't mean you're party to personal information.'

Her face cracked wide with a laugh and the film freezes.

And that's what got me. Did it really happen that way? As the months passed, I even wondered if she ever looked like I remembered. Was memory reliable to the photographic vision I had? I didn't really know anymore.

The way she seemed now was completely at odds with the way I remembered her. Physically, she seemed similar but she was not the same woman I remembered. Where were the happy times now?

My train of thought was broken by Sam, philosophy was pushed back with all the other shit into the far most recesses of my thoughts.

We had hit Mission Bay.

'Stop up here,' he said, 'good café ahead.' Sam had chosen somewhere small and chic. It was a different sort of ambience than the urban equivalent found less than two miles away. The décor had a sense of propriety that spoke of wealthy cliff top villas and swimming pools. You could have brought your kids here, decked out in designer sneakers and junior fashion-wear with scrubbed cheeks and well prepared hair. This was somewhere nice – somewhere light.

The Greek restaurant next door cast odours of moussaka and feta to waft under the nostrils of the coffee-drinking patrons. From the other side a melancholy Spanish guitar dropped notes to mingle with the smells. A Mediterranean backdrop for an Auckland vision.

'Steerforth says you're married,' Sam said.

'Used to be.'

'Kids?'

I examined the murky depths of the long black. Tan strands of aerated bubbles gripped the rim of the china white insides of the cup.

'One,' I said.

'I've got two,' Sam said. 'Boys. I only see them now and again – I send money, but you know.

Dargaville is a long way from the big smoke and their mother doesn't understand me.'

I nodded. To answer him would have meant me telling him too much. Christ, I'd only just met him. What did he want from me? He seemed a nice enough bloke, but what business of mine was it to know his details – I was certainly not going to give out mine. Instead I stared back in the cup. I felt I could make out the fine silt of the grounds drifting across the bottom. They became shifting islands, colliding and separating on indiscriminate paths.

'What split you up?' Sam said.

'Life.'

Sam looked at me expectantly, waiting for me to serve up some sort of appropriate explanation. I stared deeper into my drink, penetrating the glazed surface of the bottom, searching its porous innards and feeling its makeup.

He shrugged perhaps sensing my indifference.

'Drink up,' he said. 'I've got something to show you.'

***

We drove back to Covenant Street, parked at the end, avoiding the glow of the streetlights.

'Sometimes the shit's goes down,' Sam said. 'Aggressive bastards sometimes fly under the radar. Nothing too serious has ever happened. But you never know.'

From under his seat he pulled out a long sleek flashlight. Even in the muted darkness I saw that the knurled cylinder had weight.

'The end is lead-filled,' he said. 'Smack the pricks on the joints: knees, wrists or elbows if you get the chance. Don't hit them in the head, you don't want to kill them.'

'What if they're inside and I can't get in?'

'It breaks windows easier than limbs, eh,' Sam said, tapping a stubby finger against his temple. 'Got to use the brain as well, bro.'

The electronic chimes of Beethoven interrupted us. It came muted at first but rang free as Sam pulled the phone from his pocket. His conversation was short and terse: just a 'yeah' and 'ok'. He tossed the cell into my lap.

'It's yours,' he said. 'Keep it with you and on. Steerforth goes nuts when he can't get through.'

Jasmine said nothing when we picked her up.

'No fuck ups?' asked Sam.

All she gave back was a monotone grunt. She looked out to the distance at some far off horizon that no one else could see. The journey back seemed longer.

Even the car did not seem to cut the air like before. Rather it seemed to sail against some metaphoric wind, straining to gain purchase up Symonds Street.

When we finally parked, the BMW seemed as jaded as the beat up Toyota. Even the paintwork seemed marred by a hint of matte across the royal blue gloss. Behind my ailing car, a sleek hog was parked up, the glossy black fuel tank with orange flames gleamed dangerously in what light was available.

'Fuck,' Sam said.

'What?'

'Nothing – just business.'

Taking him at his word, I pulled at the handle to get out.

'Aren't you forgetting something?' Sam said.

I gazed back at him confused. What the hell was he going on about?

'The money, bro. Never forget the money.'

I stood outside and drew on a cigarette as the other two walked back. This wasn't a dream but somehow it felt like it. Maybe that's what it was. I could have woken up at any minute and it would all be over.

6.

This time I entered *Nymphs* through the ornate front door. An auburn-haired girl let me in, tawny-eyed and way too young. She could have been my daughter for Christ's sake. The full commercial impact of the establishment hit me as I passed through to the belly of the building.

It was like a hotel bar, a small country hotel that had been there for decades but had been slowly ignored and forgotten. Oak fittings and purple carpet lived here. Behind the counter, a forty-something bleached blonde woman stood. She had a pride-filled look of those people who were where they were supposed to be. Facing her in deep conversation perched Steerforth, his more than ample posterior balanced precariously on top of a high bar stool. This night the fucking showy prick had opted for a fashionably cut suit.

As I made my way over, a larger room to my left, opened up before me. I revised my opinion. It wasn't a hotel bar, rather it was a departure lounge with a themed hotel bar. A touch of quaintness in a garish world.

This new room was sunken floored and the perimeter was lined with long couches and low tables. Transparent long columns, liquid full with circulating air bubbles, backlit with ambient indigos, reds and emerald greens, stood to attention in each corner. Inset into the far wall was a tropical fish tank, brimming with colourful movements of life. The lighting was subdued in here. Carefully placed shadows decorated the otherwise plain walls. On the couches, five or six girls sat with two drunken looking businessmen and a nervous youth with acne scars, gazing deep into a clutched drink. He glanced quickly at me and looked into the depths of his glass again. This boy was a ship adrift. Either way, he did not seem to fit into the scene comfortably. One of the girls sidled up to him on the couch, leant in close brushing her chest on his tense arm and mumbled something into his ear.

'Alright love?' The barkeep broke my study. 'First time here?'

I turned to her as Steerforth turned on me, a slight smile dancing on his lips. 'Not this prick,' he said. 'He's your next-door neighbour, Monique. What are you having, Bill?'

'Vodka & tonic,' I said.

'What was it like – popping your cherry?'

'It seems a strange job.'

'They're all strange at the start. How was Sam?'

'Good, I like him I think. Honest seeming bloke.'

Steerforth almost spat back his drink and coughed hard. 'Steady on,' he said. 'You'll be asking him on a date next.' He indicated to the barkeep. 'Monique, Myers – Myers, Monique.'

Fucking smart prick. Led me right into that one. I had never been good at taking a joke. I swallowed my pride, concentrated on my best neutral expression and shook Monique's hand. She was older up close – the hands gave her up. Old, wrinkled skin hung about her wrists. Her fingers had a gnarled, bony touch. She smiled and became young again.

'You're smaller than I thought,' she said. 'How long have you known this reprobate?'

'Too long.'

Steerforth wrapped an arm around me and grinned back at Monique. 'We haven't changed a bit – have we, Bill?'

'I think I'm pretty much the same bloke.' In the moment, I had severe doubts about that. If I was the same I wouldn't have felt so antsy. As it happened, I was jumping out of my skin in this place. It was all so real yet at the same time contrived. Nothing in life was this easy. Still, affirmation was what the fat bastard wanted to hear.

'Sure you are,' Steerforth said, 'bit thinner on top, bit greyer, but still as ugly as ever. Drink up.'

I drank deeply, felt the ice cubes nestled against my top lip. It was a strong mix, stronger than a double, with a tang that I couldn't quite place. As the glass returned to the counter, I tried not to grimace.

'Fill him up again, Monique,' Steerforth said. Licking his lips and blowing a leery kiss,

Steerforth leant in. 'Let's meet the ladies. Bit of a perk is long overdue.'

Holding up my hand to him, I waved my disagreement. 'Not necessary, mate. I'm good.'

It was true. I had never thought about sleeping with anyone else but Jo for twenty years. It seemed like betrayal to shit on it all. That is not to say that I had never looked at another woman – never imagined what it would be like. I was no angel. But the idea of actually stepping over the line and making something of it had never crossed my mind.

'Bullshit,' Steerforth said, 'No, is not an option.'

Fuck. I was actually going to have to go through with this. My brain rallied against it, making me breathe harder. But I felt my body disagree with the brain and warm to the idea. Beneath the fabric of my trousers, I felt what was left of me harden and press against my zipper.

We wandered, drinks in hand, to the larger room and sat on a far couch. I fished for a cigarette in my jacket pocket. There were only four left. Some rationing would have to take place, before I picked up a fresh pack.

'Give us one of those,' Steerforth said. 'I've run out.'

I let out one of those silent sighs and said, 'Sure. Help yourself.'

Steerforth lit up. 'Well, who have we tonight?' He indicated to the girls lounging next to the businessmen, one of whom, could have been my auburn haired daughter. 'That's Brigitte and Lisa,' he said. 'You gents won't mind if Myers steals one of your lady friends for an hour. Do you?'

One nodded back with a shit-eating smile painted soundly on. The other looked back drunkenly. 'No,' he starts, 'we were -'

Steerforth cut him off at the pass, his voice became lower. 'I said, you won't mind if my close and personal friend, Bill, steals one of the girls for an hour.'

No reply was given. Mr Belligerence mumbled something rebellious into his drink but offered no more.

'It's alright,' I said. 'There's others. Leave these guys to themselves.'

Steerforth nodded. 'Okay,' he said, his eyes not leaving his antagonist. 'Over there is Estelle and

– I don't remember your name. What is it again, love?'

A tall brunette, vampire-like, raven hair contrasted with marble-fair skin, made even lighter by a thick foundation of makeup and set against black painted lips, smiled back. 'Morgana,' she said. She looked into my eyes and smiled with her mouth. Her eyes did not smile, instead they promised. What I didn't know – but it set my imagination running.

'Morgana,' Steerforth repeated. 'Over there with that capable looking young fella is the fair Julia.'

Julia smiled as well but it was not a convincing smile. The boy's concentration on his drink increased tenfold.

'How are you?' I said to the room in general and no one specifically. I was aware of many sets of eyes upon me. Drawing deeply on my cigarette, I created a fresh cloud in the atmosphere. Morgana's eyes were still fixed on me – they still seemed to offer something.

'Well,' Steerforth said, 'who's it to be?'

'Let's have a drink first. We've got time.'

'Not much, Myers. We're out on the town. Jasmine – get Bill a drink. Vodka & tonic.'

When had she come in? I didn't see it and I was facing the door. Maybe it was Morgana's perusal that diverted my attention – either that or she was some sort of ghost. She was skinny enough.

Jasmine nodded and left, did not look at me when she returned, even when she placed my vodka on the low table.

'What about Jasmine? She's a good girl.'

'No, I don't think so.'

Her shoulders drained of tension.

'Well, who then?' Steerforth asked.

I looked at Morgana, whose eyes were still trained on me. 'How about you?' I said. 'Do you want to?'

'Of course she wants to,' Steerforth said, 'she's on the payroll.' He nodded at Morgana. 'Take him through. See Monique about what room. Only the best service.'

'Naturally,' Morgana purred. She led me to the bar. Steerforth followed close behind.

'Just the hour?' Monique asked, looking beyond me at Steerforth. He must have nodded because she carried on at some unseen agreement. 'Take him through to the Egyptian Room.'

As we left, I heard Steerforth saying to Monique. 'Get those suits out of here. Tell them that they're too pissed or something. Smart arses.'

'They've got cash. Business is slow tonight and you know who's upstairs.'

'I don't fucking care. It's my business – not anyone else's.'

'Best no one else hears that.'

The conversation faded away into white noise the further we moved away. Apparently, Steerforth was not the total king of his castle.

We travelled the passageway and Morgana's arm encircled my waist. She chose the first door we came to, opened it for me and let me in.

'Why don't you take a shower,' she said. 'There's a towel on the chair. Want another drink?'

Thinking of the quick vodkas I had already had, I decide. 'No. I'll be fine.'

Alone, I noticed for the first time the room around me. Plainer than its Antoinette companion, it displayed a large print of Horus with a crook and flail crossed over the top and screwed into the far wall. It was enclosed by a panelled mirror. The effect was that of a room twice its actual size with a rectangular bed. My reflection was fragmented by the mirror, sectioned off into perpendicular compartments. A thick line of bisection ran perfectly from the centre of my crown, through my crotch to halve my legs. The face that stared back at me was not symmetrical. One eye sat lower than the other. I had never noticed this blemish before; the lack of an axis to see it in an ordinary mirror had fooled me since birth. My beak of a nose proved to be flawed as well. A lump on the left – or was it the right – was not reflected on the other side. I had always suspected this but I had never closely examined the phenomena before. Jesus, I belonged in a cathedral in Notre Dame all that was missing was the rags and the stick-on hump. How did she manage to wake up to me all those years and not be sick? Wonders never ceased.

I took off my jacket and placed it over the back of the simple wooden chair with the towel placed on it. The squarish appearance of my shoulders was reduced to gentle slopes by the rayon shirt. I unbuttoned it and noticed again the greyish patchwork of chest hair. It was harder to deal with than the grey on my head. Up there it was distinguished – down here and further below was just old.

Thinner than I was months ago too, but the same amount of skin seemed to remain. The chest had slipped, over the years, into two hairy breasts; the line of my abdomen seemed lax and misshapen. Pulling off the rest of my clothes, I stood and looked at my final glorious transformation. The body that launched a thousand ships – all bouncing off the top of the waves to get the fuck out of there. I sighed, opened the shower stall door, turned the faucet and stepped inside.

Rivulets of steam-drenched water washed their way through what was left of my hair and ran over my closed eyes and dropped to the drain. The heat elevated my heart rate. I examined the rays of light that had pierced the thin skin of my closed lids. They danced in ever-changing pinpoints, alternating slightly in colour and shifting in origin.

I heard the door close and the rustle of movement beyond. My cock stood at attention. Despite myself, I find this exciting.

The shower stall opened with a clack. I opened my eyes and she was there, naked, sinuous, her eyes still promising the world. Two coiling snakes: emerald and gold scaled, were wound in tattoos up both thighs. Spiralling around her buttocks, the fanged heads converged at the top of the pubis, split tongues pointed the way.

'Comfortable?' she asked.

'Fine.'

She reached behind me, plucked a cake of alabaster soap from the recessed holder and washed me down in slow, measured strokes. The eyes still promised. She chose my chest first. I closed my eyes thinking of the grey scourge upon it. Her caress lowered, finding its way home.

'Nice cock,' she said. 'I prefer a circumcised cock. They're cleaner.'

'You've said that before.'

Morgana closed her eyes, as if in thought. 'No,' she said finally. 'It gets to the point where you don't notice so much. You haven't pawed at me.' She gave my cock a quick squeeze. 'I know you want to. You're sort of polite, so I noticed. No big deal.'

'I haven't paid for it before.'

'You aren't now. Moneybags is. Rinse off and I'll dry you.'

She worked at me with the towel in much the same way she did with the soap. I was fucking horny now, despite all my protests. The mind held a truce with my body. Morgana led me to the bed and got me to lie face down.

The touch of her fingers kneading the knots in my back was not what relaxed me. It was her smell. Months – maybe even longer – had passed since I had smelt the essence of a woman. As she slid her front along the length of my back, the scent drew closer, became more potent. I had missed this. The possibilities that lay before me came jumbled and fast as she turned me over.

Her body slid languidly up me, mimicking the path of her ink-stained serpents. I gasped as my cock temporarily split her breasts and disappeared from sight to the depths of her belly. Morgana's eyes were closed. I did the same.

'Thinking of your wife?' she said.

'I'm not married.'

The cool touch of her fingers enveloped my wrist. 'Your finger tells a different story,' she said.

'I haven't got around to taking it of yet.'

'Oh,' she said. 'Naughty boy.'

Opening my eyes, I saw her looking down on me. The light overhead cast a halo around her face. It placed her in soft focus. Morgana reached above me and pulled a foiled condom packet into sight. Tearing it open, she slipped its contents over me.

'Give me a minute,' she said. 'I hate the taste of these things.'

'You don't have to if you don't want to.'

Her smile became real. She knelt astride me then lowered herself slowly onto me. The vampire skin turned to liquid heat behind the thin veil of latex.

'What about if I want to,' she said. 'It's a nice cock after all. Maybe you're just in a hurry to fuck me.'

I looked up at the ceiling, panelled mirror as well. It bubbled and shifted – what the fuck was going on with my head? I was watching myself in my own personal porno. Morgana's body seemed to have melded with mine. We had become a union of skin – one fleshy, heaving beast. The serpents on her legs appeared to slither forth. I felt the dry rasp of their scales wrap around my own thighs, as she moved on me, entwined me, securing the shackles of our new form

'You ok?' she said.

The lines of her face seemed longer and more drawn. I imagined that I saw the faint pulse of blood in the veins of her eyes. Morgana bent her face to my chest and traced her tongue slowly over my nipple. I arched my back and cried as I felt the sharp sensation of her teeth as she bit me lightly.

Fuck me, I'd come. I was a premature ejaculator – a bloody two stroke. My cheeks burned and I closed my eyes. *Good one Romeo.* Why was my head spinning still? What the fuck was going on with me?

'I'm sorry,' I said. 'Hasn't happened like that before. I feel sort of strange.'

'You're not the first it's happened to. You won't be the last. Relax, I don't care.'

'Really. I do feel fucking weird.'

I was not lying. I did. For all I knew I was in the first stages of a heart attack. That couldn't happen. I had things to see through.

'Listen honey,' she said. 'I fuck for a living. You're doing me a favour by being quick.'

Her eyes did not promise anything anymore, they merely looked annoyed. They seemed to soften after a bit, maybe with empathy.

'We can try again,' she said, 'if you want. I don't normally but you seem nice.'

Knowing my luck, I knew I would either not be able to get it up – or worse – repeat the whole pitiful performance over again. Fuck that, it was better off to find some excuse.

'No,' I said. 'Can't we just lie down for a bit? I'm an old man after all.'

Morgana snorted. 'Sure.' She nestled into me. I was only half telling the truth. I wanted to hold onto her scent.

We lay in silence for maybe minutes or maybe only short seconds. I was comfortable in the position. If I closed my eyes and thought of Levin, perhaps I would have travelled back for good. But that could never happen.

'We better get up,' Morgana said eventually. 'They'll want the room soon.'

As I dressed, she straightened the bed and meticulously folded a towel into a pink scalloped arrangement on top of the covers. She was still cleaning when I left.

'Want some advice?' she said, as I opened the door.

'What?'

'Get out of here while you can. You're too small and that fat bastard has got trouble on the horizon.'

'You bet he has,' I replied, as I closed the door behind me.

Walking back down the passage was like swimming through oil. My mind was moving as quickly and erratically as my heartbeat, yet my body travelled slowly. I met Steerforth halfway down, not noticing him come up on me. His suit shimmered upon him.

'All good?' he asked.

'Fine.'

'How are you feeling?'

'Funny you should say that. Fucking strange. I think I'm coming down with something.'

Steerforth cracked a smile. 'I got Monique to slip you a cocktail. You're not sleeping on me tonight.'

7.

'What did you give me?'

'Relax, nothing that'll kill you. No, heart problems, have you?'

The pumping that pounded the inside of my ribs vented its frustration. 'You could have fucking asked me. Christ, I thought I was having a heart attack or something.

'What the hell -' I spluttered

'Relax -'

'- did you think you were doing?'

'- just go with it. Harden up.'

'What?' I felt my voice ascend a couple of octaves. The situation was hyperreal. The passageway around us reached away in perfect perspective; the doors were inky-deep mouths that threatened to swallow it all up in hungry gulps. Steerforth's suit still shimmered, but the contours of his face that sat on top were a stark relief.

I fancied I could see into the very pores of his skin and break through to the latticework of small, angry veins that were splayed across his nose. The diamond stud in his ear that merely glistened before now glared at me with its opulent meanness. And over it all I sensed the presence of grime, barely visible, but hidden in his eyes.

'Calm down, Bill,' Steerforth said. 'We're old mates, remember? Just having a good time – just like the old days. That's what you're up for, isn't it?'

Although my conscience battled against it, I forced my mouth in a semblance of a smile. As I felt Steerforth's eyes probe my own, I tried to reflect the lies my mouth told. 'Sorry, mate,' I said. 'I just freaked out. You could have told me.'

Steerforth didn't answer for a moment, instead he continued to probe my face. What could he see there? If I had given anything away, I may as well have got back into the car and driven away. But his look seemed only one of appraisal.

'Where would have been the fun in that?' Steerforth said, 'You get riled up, don't you.'

'Just caught by surprise that's all.' I did not know if I was still being lucid. It seemed I was, but I was not in sync with myself. Doubts began to cloud over the peripheries, gnawing at me.

Steerforth grinned, stretched forward and placed me in a headlock.

'Fuck you're a worry, boy.'

An impending sense of claustrophobia hit me. I struggled against him. I twisted with him and eased my head out.

He let me go and I emerged from the sweat of his deodorant unscathed and still in control. The room still undulated and careered. I'm wasn't sure, but I was fairly certain that the patches of wall, just beyond my sight, were slowly dripping onto the carpet. Quickly I turned to see if it was true, but the walls stood still and proved me wrong.

'C'mon,' Steerforth said, 'we got things to do.'

The journey back seemed to take forever. It was still a walk through oil, languid slow and soaked with damp friction. Steerforth was talking to me but I was unable to decipher it. It was an amusing sentiment because he was laughing at some notion. I found myself returning his laughter, though for the life of me I could not see why. I was serious on the inside – that much I knew. But all that emotion was cloaked in a blanket of comedy. It was all mouth and trousers with no legs. That thought tipped the balance and I collapsed against a soft wall and laughed. It was uncontrollable – I couldn't breathe, trapped as I was in my own mirth. Steerforth was laughing as well. At me.

A door opened further down the hall. An old guy with a bald head, naked except for a towel emerged. His tits were larger and hairier than mine. He waddled towards the lounge on needle-thin chicken legs. The sight sent me deeper. If I didn't stop soon I was going to do some damage to myself. Then what use would I have been?

Steerforth grabbed me by the arm, pushed his face close to mine and spoke. It took a moment to decipher the message. The static charge across my synapses must have taken a slow boat. 'Get a grip, Bill. Big night ahead,' he said.

The message seeped in and we finally made it to the bright lights of the lounge.

And bright they were, startling, seemingly more lurid than before, intense and in a way more brazen. There were fewer girls than before - Jasmine and another whose name escaped me – and not a patron in sight. I hoped the young fella went through. He looked like he needed it and to be selfish, it meant there was someone here more inept than myself at this game. We sat on an available couch. There were plenty of available couches.

'Another drink and we're off,' Steerforth said. Big night ahead, boy.'

Steerforth abandoned me. I looked over at Jasmine who was looking at everything but me. What was it about her? I hadn't been rude – treated her badly. In fact, I had gone out of my way not to acknowledge her at all. But even my avoidance was seen in an awful light. Maybe I had done something. Perhaps it was paranoia, but I got the distinct feeling I had transgressed her in some way. I leant forward.

'Why don't you like me?'

It was as if I didn't exist. The ambience of the room seemed to be more to her liking than an old fart like me.

'I said: why don't you like me?'

It seemed to me that more than a year passed. She still didn't look at me but words deigned to cross her lips. 'I'm not paid to like you.'

Sitting back, my detached mind mulled it over. It still teetered in and out but the focus of the dilemma balanced it somewhat. Even this rationale was lost as Steerforth reappeared with two doubles. He flopped himself next to me – the weight distribution of the couch tipped in his favour. 'Not falling in love?' he asked. 'She's my special girl – my real special girl. Aren't you, sweetness?'

The carpet caught her attention. Was that a brief shudder I detected? Perhaps or perhaps not. I was too far gone to decide – or care. Didn't like me anyway. An inkling of a thought crossed my mind, that the carpet must have been as compelling as the décor to her. An unsuppressed chortle forced its way from my stomach. I contained it – wasn't going down that route again.

Monique appeared at the entrance, winked at me, straightened her face and looked at Steerforth. 'Looks like your night's off,' she said. 'Tama wants you upstairs.'

'Can't it wait?'

'No. You know what those two are like when they get together. It'll be all business.'

Steerforth's lips set themselves in a firm line. 'Tell them I'll be up,' he said. He drained the contents of his glass and slammed it down on the table. 'Probably nothing. I'll be down in a minute. Make sure you've got your party shoes on.' As he left, two familiar businessmen arrived with wet hair and each with a girl in tow. It seemed to me that a maroon tide rose from Steerforth's shirt collar to rest on his brow. He glared at Monique and clenched his hammy fists.

'What the hell are these two pricks still here for? What did I tell you?'

'Sam said that we can't afford to turn away paying customers. He said you of all people should know that.'

The maroon transformed into an iridescent crimson. 'Who the fuck is running this show?'

Monique said nothing, merely raised a querulous eyebrow at him. Steerforth turned on his victims. 'And what the fuck are you looking at?'

Mr Belligerence now looked subordinate. Still he mustered the courage to reply. 'Nothing, mate. We don't want any trouble – we'll go. The other guy said it was cool – we'll just go.'

'That's right,' Steerforth said. 'Fuck off.'

The aggression of Steerforth hit me metaphysically. I could actually feel myself squirming deeper into the back of the couch. Jasmine had disappeared. How the fuck did she do that? I wasn't scared. I had seen angry men before. Just go to any public bar around closing time. But I had always had the ability to blend into the background. Here I stuck out like a hazard light.

'Right,' Steerforth said, 'I'm going to sort those pricks out upstairs.' He pushed past Monique who was paler and seemed to have become one with the doorframe. A loud silence entered the space and the colours seemed to dim with his passing.

Another year passed until Mr Belligerence lets out his breath. 'I'm sorry,' he said. He turned to his silent companion. 'Let's go.'

'Don't worry about him,' said Monique, 'he will have forgotten everything tomorrow. Don't let it stop you coming again. I'll walk you out.'

'No offence, but I came here to escape that sort of shit. We'll see ourselves out.'

They passed from sight. Monique sat herself next to me. She rubbed my shoulder with a warm friendly hand. 'How about you?' she said. 'Sorry about the drink, but you just have to go along with his games – wherever they lead you. Can't argue with that man.'

She slipped a small white pill into my hand. I must look at her strangely because she said, 'It's a sedative. They help me sleep during the day. I have been doing this for years but I still can't adjust my body clock. It'll take the edge off you – calm you down a bit.'

I downed the pill with a bitter swallow of vodka. It burned the back of my throat.

Steerforth's games. Life, I supposed, had become a game for me as well. No responsibility anymore. No caring. Nothing of anything. The thought amused me. I stifled another laugh – when would the sedative kick in? Soon I hoped.

'Are you ok?' Monique said.

I laughed at her. It sounded ugly to my ears. 'Fine. I haven't been better in months.'

'Right,' she said and edged away from me, slowly like a victim.

The sick grin I felt plastered on my face did not reflect my turmoil. I didn't like offending people and I had upset her. Not as far as hurting her, but I certainly made her feel uneasy. Somehow that was worse. Monique got up quietly and left.

Loneliness fell on me heavy. The solitude of my room beckoned me – if only for minutes.

I rose from my perch. It felt as if the couch rose with me momentarily and then fell in a slow dollop. Wandering through to the bar, I spotted Monique cleaning glasses behind her oak wall.

'I'm off, mother,' I said. 'Tell father I'm in my room. Won't be long.'

Monique just looked back at me, not in an unfriendly way, rather with a pitying look of a mother at a wayward child beyond her control.

I made it all the way up the stairs to the velvet lady. She seemed sad, as if forced to stand there provocatively on the wall. I ran my finger down her cheek, brushed her imaginary tears away.

She looked at my door. I imagined her whispering, *'Hurry.'*

My hand turned the key and grabbed the handle.

'Where the fuck are you going?' Steerforth said, stamping down the passage. He had left me with crimson cheeks and bluster – he returned wraith-like white, his anger contained behind set lips.

'I needed some time.'

Steerforth stepped forward and pushed me hard against the door. Slipping, I hit the floor. 'What the hell answer is that,' he roared. 'You think this is some sort of a joke. I invite you out of the kindness of my heart into my home and all you do is give me shit.'

He stood over me, grabbed me by the shirtfront and hauled me up. My collar tightened cutting my lungs from much needed air. Angry, white spots swarmed like bees in front of my eyes. Beyond me, Steerforth's fat face simmered. Panic set in, but from far away. My vision blurred and I felt the load of consciousness begin to swim away. I dropped to the ground suddenly and violently. Looking up I saw Steerforth in the grasp of Sam.

Whereas Steerforth was flailing passion, Sam was an emotionless vice. I had never thought of Steerforth as small – even when we were kids – but he looked tiny in the moment. It was not a lack of height or girth that made him this way. It was the battle of wills.

'Get the fuck off me, you...'

'Careful, Alan,' Sam said, 'don't be saying shit you might regret.'

'Don't call me, Alan,' Steerforth said.

'I'm sorry, but you can't play up here. It's not Bill's fault. It's just business – you know that. Sort it out and we'll be good.'

Steerforth seemed to calm himself. Sam loosened his grip only to be subjected to a new attack. 'Fucking let me go,' Steerforth said.

Sam pushed his face closer. 'You know who's in the office,' he hissed. 'Don't fuck up.'

Looking down the hall, I saw framed in the office door a leather-clad figure. He seemed to be Sam in miniature. Same face, same shape, just kilos lighter and inches shorter. The resemblance was striking. He looked back at me then retreated closing the door behind him.

'Come on Steerforth, let's get out of here,' I said.

It was like flicking a light switch off. The tension left Steerforth's body.

'Yeah,' he said, 'let's go. You can earn me some fucking money instead of spending it.' He shrugged himself out of Sam's grip, as if announcing to the empty passage that he had somehow won. Stamping away towards the stairs he called, 'You coming or what?'

Resigned, I started to follow him.

'Good on you, bro,' Sam said. 'Pick you up tomorrow morning.'

'What for?'

'For Christ's sake,' Steerforth moaned from the stairwell.

'Get you some threads – remember?' Sam said.

I didn't remember but I nodded to him anyway. Following the path of Steerforth, I met him downstairs by the car. The winter night was awash with in drizzle. The melancholy of it slowed my heart. Hopefully Monique's little pill had started to do its work.

'Kissing your new friend goodbye?' Steerforth said.

'Just sorting out the job.'

'You're working for me not that arsehole.'

'I can't drive,' I said, changing the subject.

'What?'

'I can't drive. I'm too fucked up.'

'Useless prick,' he said, 'that's your bloody job. Give us the keys.'

He snatched them from me. 'Get in the car,' he said. 'You're on the job now. No fucking around.'

As I shut the door, the wheels were already moving. He barely avoided the low-slung Harley. We skidded on the gravel until the rubber bit the asphalt surface of Sandringham Road.

8.

The passenger seat shrouded me. It was like sitting in a massive, gloved hand. We were on a network of streets leading to the New North Road. Even in daytime, when I used to live here, this latticework of road and concrete was a source of confusion. I always used to get the sense that I was forever turning the wrong corner. No right-angled intersections to make it easy. This night, with the rhythmical blaze of street lamp and light reflecting from the damp surfaces, my perplexity was complete.

Steerforth had no trouble navigating the course. He gripped the steering wheel in silence and his expression sat like a storm cloud amid the elegant interior of the car. Although it was dark, I fancied that the points of Steerforth's knuckles had turned white due to the intensity of his grasp.

As we stopped at some red lights on New North Road, I looked out to my left at the beginning of the Kingsland shops. It all looked familiar but at the same time different. This place used to be a shit hole. Maybe it was the way the sodium vapour lights overhead threw their rays off the glass fronts of the buildings. Or the hint of fresh paint over the facades, but there was a definite air of respectability about the place. It didn't look dangerous the way it used to.

Not the transitional youth of Karangahape Road, but more of a rebirth – a baby face with an old person's eyes.

'The place I knew is dead,' I murmured to no one in particular.

'For Christ's sake,' Steerforth said. He punched the stereo on.

The sounds that blared from the speakers were an exercise in harshness. It was manufactured white noise, sectioned off with brief lulls, many times a second. The thrum of the beats asserted a monotonous rhythm.

The voice that sat above it all was distorted and without inflection. It chanted a pseudo-mantra that was without meaning. Through it I picked out the words 'suck' and 'soul'. I experienced the power of sibilance, soft edged consonants running together piercing the aural senses.

Red light changed to green light and the car started once more on its course. We turned left opposite a petrol station and descended a steep road. From the top, I spied the North-Western motorway imbued with a halo. The effect of car headlights, the drizzle and a forming mist at ground level.

The pit of my stomach was left behind at the prow of the rise. It was not until we hit the bottom of the cul-de-sac ending, that it returned homeward.

With the turn of the key, the music ceased and only the bee-like drone of the cars on the motorway could be heard. From our position at the bottom, I could no longer see the North-Western. Rather it sat prominent on a proud lip, beyond our sight on the undeveloped chin of our parking spot.

'What are you waiting for?' Steerforth said.

'What do you mean?'

'Get in there.'

'Where?'

'Over there.' He pointed at a shabby, dilapidated house. Without closely inspecting it, I knew of the slow, creeping rot that resided in the foundation, the floors that sat at a permanent lean; the weatherboards that no longer married up against each other. It was a sick house, terminally ill, waiting for the release of death.

'What do you want me to do?'

'Go get him.'

'Who?'

'Jesus, your saviour,' Steerforth said with a beast grin. 'Ask for Morty – he'll be coming with us.'

'I don't know him.'

'So what. I'm paying you aren't I? Off you go.'

There was something about his tone, that smugness that worried me. He was up to something. Probably some vicious dog behind the gate, ready to come at me as far as the chain would let it. Maybe it was nothing. But this man has drugged and choked me. I was definitely wary of him. Fat bastard.

Getting out the passenger side, I started across the deserted road. Turning back halfway across, I looked back at him. He waved me on with a smile. His teeth shone in the gloom.

The rotten nature of the dwelling increased with each step I took. Grasses at the front grew wild and unfettered. Even the footpath that passed it by was uneven and cracked. The fence – picketed and probably at some time a desirable, sellable feature – was missing palings. It was a wide broken mouth set in a fixed rigid grin, the gaps revealing long, poisoned gums of concrete. Through the gaps I saw a bicycle lying dormant on its side, its front wheel immersed in a dark puddle. It seemed a dead, ancient beast – the puddle, the blood of the kill. No sign of a dog. Maybe I was paranoid.

The mouldering gate had to be physically lifted to open so access could be gained. The door itself was decrepit. Its face contained two long panels of stained glass – one intact, one not. The damaged pane had a pinpoint hole from which cracks spread in a haphazard web outwards. Behind it a nailed piece of plywood was apparently holding the flaws together in a rough compress. It was quiet inside. Only the hint of light beyond spoke of any life present.

Before I knocked, I looked back at the BMW. Only the quick flare of a lighter, then the faint ember of a cigarette tip announced Steerforth's presence. *What's going on in that head of yours, Alan?* The thud of my heartbeat became apparent once more.

Turning back to the door, I raised my hand to knock. Before my knuckles dropped it opened.

It was a clothed, skeletal figure that answered, attired in a threadbare corduroy blazer and drainpipe-shaped trousers all sat on top of chrome tipped boots. He wore a jaundice-yellow face, the skin stretched like parchment over brutish bones. If his bone structure were fine, the vision before me would be palatable. However this was a strong face and the amount of flesh applied to it was at odds with the canvas it sat upon.

'Who are you?' he asked.

'I've come to get Morty.'

Shit. It sounded like I was picking him up for a date. I should have bought a corsage and chocolates. Laughter bubbled once more. Monique's sedative wasn't as strong as I had thought.

'Do I know you?'

'No.'

His face cracked a smile. He looked like a vampire, the cold, sterile look of Christopher Lee, not the fleshy entity that was Lugosi.

'I'm sorry,' he said, 'you can't be too careful these days. He's in the lounge. Come in.'

Holding the door ajar, he let me through. I heard the door close behind me, almost at the same time as I felt a sharp kick at the fulcrum point behind my knee. All I could do was fall flat on my face, my hands not quick enough to stop it cracking against the grubby floorboards. My nose didn't crack but I felt it blow up. As I lay prone, he directed two hard blows to my kidneys, jumped across my back and grabbed my hair from the front of my head and forced my skull and vertebrae back at an awkward angle. I was in real pain and effectively couldn't move without hurting myself more.

'This isn't an exact science,' he said calmly, 'but I'm pretty sure if I pull back hard enough I can do you considerable damage – maybe even paralyse you. So I will ask you a few questions and you will answer them. Why are you here?'

'What -'

My head was rammed hard against the floor. For the second time tonight my vision blurred – this time with tears brought on by a swollen nose.

'I'm sorry. Maybe you don't get it. I ask the questions and you tell me the answer. Why are you here?'

'To pick up Morty.'

'Who's Morty?'

'I've no idea.'

'Then why -'

A loud crashing at the door interrupted us. I heard Steerforth's smug voice, 'It's ok, Morty. Let me in.'

The unseen fingers released my hair and again my head smacked the boards. My face felt swollen up, my nose I was sure was a pomegranate. I rolled over slowly to see Morty open the door and the rolling, smirking bulk of Steerforth entered.

'I see you two have been getting acquainted,' Steerforth said. 'Morty this is Bill – you'll like him I think. He reminds me of you.'

Slowly, I pushed myself to my feet. Too tired and sore to get angry, I extended my hand to Morty. He didn't attempt to reciprocate instead he stared back deadpan.

'I don't know you,' Morty said, 'so you can call me Mr Mortimer.' Turning to Steerforth he said, 'Got my money, Alan?'

Steerforth reached into his jacket and pulled an envelope from an inside pocket. 'You don't have to ask that, Morty -'

Morty held his palm up for silence. 'Business first,' he said. Ripping open the envelope, he counted out the hundred dollar bills. I estimated there were about seven or eight inside. With a look of satisfaction, Morty pocketed the bills and gestured to us. 'Come through,' he said, 'I've a few thing to do before we go.'

'See, he talks like you. All fucked up and posh. Shit, he even looks the same.'

What the hell was Steerforth talking about? I wasn't this fucking thug. I thought chemicals had addled Steerforth's brain if he saw any similarities between us.

We moved down a short passage with a high ceiling, into what could only be loosely described as a living room, because who the hell in their right mind would choose to live in such a space? It was a green polyester couch, without legs where there should be, a small radio on a beer crate and a single picture.

A Van Gogh print. A rural town at night being swallowed by a ravenous moon and stars. The sky was an angry sea: waves of colour struck outwards from the pinpoints of light. The sky crashed against a lonely landscape, only a wild clump of fauna stood in defiance. The lines of shaded buildings are pulled askew by the weight of the cosmos. *Starry Night*. Not a good title. The emotion of the work was darker than that.

The rest of the walls were bare beige, water stained in patches and dank. In one corner the ceiling sagged dangerously and a distinct odour of mildew permeated everything.

'I've said this before, Morty,' Steerforth said, 'with all the dosh you earn, why don't you get yourself some decent gear?'

'As I've told you, Alan, one becomes too attached to possessions. The more one owns, the greater the addiction. It all depreciates each day – so why bother. Everything becomes an unbreakable burden. Therefore I choose not to own, merely use what is at hand when I need it, or rent it when I desire it. That way the connection is temporary and detached and I remain free, for the most part.'

There was nothing wrong with Morty's philosophy. In fact, there was a lot in it that I agreed with. But from his lips it had a bitter, citrus twist. Perhaps it was sour grapes at the way he had just used my head as a basketball. No, it was more than that.

'What about the painting,' I said. 'Isn't that an unnecessary asset?'

'That's just a reflection of my ideas,' Morty said.

It was all vaguely repellent. Examining the night scene again, I saw that the beige paper that surrounded it was flyblown. It gave the darker colours inside a sickly sheen.

'Wait here,' Morty said. 'I'll get ready.' He left silently, the only sound, a door closing down the passage. Steerforth dug me in the ribs with his elbow. I winced – it had been a hard night.

'What did I say?' he said. 'It's uncanny.'

'What?'

'You two – peas in a pod.'

'Sorry, I don't see it.'

'You're joking...'

'Whatever...'

Shaking my head I pulled a cigarette out. One left. Placing it in my mouth, I searched my jacket for a lighter. There wasn't one. I found it in my trousers – in the left pocket. It was always in the left pocket. I struck the flint.

'Can't smoke in here,' Steerforth whispered.

'Doesn't he smoke?'

'Yeah. You just can't smoke in here – he doesn't like it.'

Annoyed, I stuffed it back into the packet, timing it perfectly with Morty's return.

'Let's get on with it,' he said.

As we passed back through the front door, Morty asked, 'You didn't smoke did you?'

'No.'

'I thought I smelt it. I can't stand the smell of burnt tobacco inside. It's an outdoor habit.'

At the car Steerforth piped in, 'You get in the back, Myers. Mr Mortimer will sit up front with me.'

'You get to call me Morty, Alan. One name's all you get of me.'

'Sorry Morty.'

We got in and u-turned back up and turn towards the city's heart.

'Where are we going?' I asked.

'Visiting a friend, Myers. Visiting a friend.'

9.

We drove down Symonds Street. Steerforth turned the stereo back on. Morty switched it off. 'Noise pollution is as bad as physical rubbish,' he said.

Not a peep from Steerforth in response.

Our trip continued in silence. I looked down on the silhouettes of unsightly cranes made impressive at night by illuminating signage. Office windows were still alive past the respectable hours of business. I saw the city centre as a neon heart pumping the means of industry. We turned left into a small side road just above the university. Apart from cars parked indiscriminately on either side, there was no apparent life abroad. Steerforth scraped the tires against the kerb as he parked up and looked across the front seats at Morty.

'Coming in?'

'Probably smokers in there, Alan,' Morty said. 'Best you bring the work to me. It's only a small job after all.'

'Looks like you and me, Bill,' Steerforth said.

We got out, Steerforth from the comfort of the driver's side, me from the depths of the back seat. I pushed myself out hard – difficult to exit a car on a slope.

As soon as I hit the fresh air, a sense of calm came over me. Perhaps it was the stillness of the avenue, the gaunt buildings and the cars themselves. They were the street's only inhabitants. I was glad to get away from the sociopath that sat in the passenger seat. He gave scary a whole new slant. The less I was around him the better. And Steerforth thought I was like him? Fuck that.

'Where to,' I asked.

'Up in the *Deloitte Building*,' said Steerforth, pointing at the edifice next-door.

'What's up there?'

'What do you think?' We entered the dimly lit foyer and climbed a steep staircase. Not plushly floored, like the stairs to my place, instead it was green linoleum covered with walls of butter yellow. It was the sort of building it looked and felt like, no depth of style and no sense of chic. We arrived at a set of double doors – number 213 on one side and a small brass plaque saying, *Cupids* on the other– with a white and black buzzer at the side, Steerforth steeled his face and pressed for entry. Above us, where ceiling met wall, underneath a tinted Perspex dome, a camera was positioned. The faint glow of a light tells me that it was active. There was no signage to say what went on behind the pine veneer but it did not take much imagination.

No one answered. Steerforth pushed the buzzer again, this time aggressively for long seconds. Still no reply. He pushed again, leaving his finger pushed down until finally the door opened a crack, then to its fullest extent.

A girl, possibly Thai or maybe from somewhere further south-east answered. She's pretty, her head barely reaching my chest, 'Come in, come in.' she said.

Steerforth pushed past her, ignoring her delicate presence. I followed him in, but afforded her the courtesy of a smile. We stood in a partitioned section of a larger room; another small exit waited in front. There was no one present besides our hostess and us.

'Where's your boss?' Steerforth said.

'Brian?' She made the 'r' into a soft 'w'.

'Yeah, Brian. How many bosses you got?'

She looked confused. Steerforth's question had beaten her ability to translate. *Where do you go to learn sarcasm?* Bowing her head slightly, she assumed a look of concentration as if thinking of a suitable answer.

'He's not here, Steerforth,' a woman's voice called from beyond the partitioning. 'He's down at the club.'

The voice stepped into view in the form of a redhead – a strawberry blonde – with a pale complexion, without makeup and without the smattering of freckles that usually accompanied that particular hair colour. She must have been thirty or so – it was so hard to tell these days. Good looking too. Not in the classical sense, but there was character there. She wore her flaws as a badge.

Steerforth leered. 'Hey, Cat,' he said, 'when are you going to leave this shithole and work for me?'

Cat beamed a saccharine grin. 'Swap one dump for another, you mean? Brian's alright in his own way and besides, I heard you were on the way out?'

'Who told you that? You're not fucking him are you – you could do better.'

'Who? You?'

'Why not? I'm a cuddly sort. More cushion for the pushin'.'

She let out a snort – one part humour, one part derision and one part I didn't know.

'So he's at the club then?' Steerforth said.

'That's what I said.'

'I'll come back if he's not.'

Her eyes fell on me. They were cornflower blue rimmed with a darker hue. 'If you do, bring your friend. He's a cutie.'

Steerforth's mouth tightened. 'He couldn't afford you.'

'Says who?' I said.

'I fucking do,' Steerforth said. 'Now, get your arse downstairs. You're on my time.'

As I left I heard Cat call after me, 'Bye tiger, be seeing you.'

The Asian girl shrunk from me as I moved past her.

**

I hit the bottom floor and heard the tumble of Steerforth behind me. He caught up, slightly breathless. As we hit the road he said to me, 'You cutting my lunch?'

'What?'

'You know what I mean...Cat.'

'I don't know what you mean.'

'Just don't be sniffing around her. She's off limits. Get it? Fucking hell, I already got you laid tonight.'

'I didn't even talk to her.'

'Let's just keep it that way. Keep your mind on the job.'

Disgruntled, I got back into the car.

As Steerforth shut his door, Morty piped in, 'Not there then?'

'No kidding,' Steerforth replied, 'He's at the other place, downtown.'

'If this goes on too long you going to have to pay,' said Morty, 'I'm running the clock, remember.'

'You'll get your fucking money.'

'You're not losing your temper with me, are you, Alan? You know that's just wasted energy on you part. Better you vent it on something or someone more deserving. Isn't that right, Bill?' Morty said, looking in the direction of the backseat.

'Yeah.'

'Sorry Morty,' said Steerforth, 'I'm just a bit hyped, that's all.'

The road was too narrow to turn around; instead we implemented a five point turn. We headed up and down towards the waterfront.

***

Customs Street was well lit, a blend of people walked the pavements. The rich in search of fun in chrome-plated bars and neon lights and the ordinary, unable to gain access there, drifted slightly west to the diminishing seedier bars and strip clubs of Fort Street and its accompanying short brothers and sisters. We turned illegally into the dead-end side of Fort Street and parked behind a row of dead and gone buildings.

'You shouldn't have done that, Alan,' Morty said, 'in our line of business, we don't want to attract the attention of the law. If we do, the jobs off for me with pay.'

Steerforth did not reply and switched the engine off. 'I suppose you'll be waiting here for us?' he asked.

'Don't be too long, Alan,' Morty said. 'This is a well-watched part of town. Video cameras everywhere. Best to get it over with quick.'

Again Steerforth and I exited the vehicle, walked to the encroaching road, round the corner and stopped outside a sparking neon sign. A fluorescent pink woman, with glowing red nipples and a flashing, winking eye. The signage above her announced her name: *The Redlight Club*. On the door, stood a behemoth bouncer, Pacific Islander and a smaller European counterpart. The look in the smaller man's eye did not have the surety of his companion. He shifted left and right, sizing us up, unsure of his position. His partner was uncaring, deadpan and confident.

'Hey George,' said Steerforth, 'is he in there? They told us we could find him here at the other place.'

'Yeah,' said George, 'the boss said you'd be coming.'

They moved towards the entrance. The apprentice monkey said quickly, 'That'll be ten bucks each.'

'I don't think so, brother,' said Steerforth and continued his advance forward, 'Isn't that right, George.'

George said to his companion, 'It's alright, Steerforth's a friend.'

'Yeah,' said Steerforth, pushing his nose close to the itinerant bouncer, 'a friend.'

We walked inside to the room I expected. It was smoky and only half-full. Its centre consisted of an elevated runway, carpeted with two poles at either end. On one a girl gyrated half-heartedly against its length, the music did not reflect the tired state she was in. A few catcalls broke over the top of the sound as she spread herself on the floor in front of a drunken table. She held her pussy aloft, inches from the floor, just out of reach. No tips forthcoming she strutted down the runway towards the other pole. A few feet from it, she leapt, taking me by surprise. She landed gracefully halfway up its length, swung around twice and alighted once more on to the carpet and looked directly at me standing stationary before her.

It seems she looked deep into my eyes, beyond the retinas and into my mind. Placing an index finger into her mouth, she sucked it off leisurely, withdrew it, placed it on her clit and rubbed it with an exaggerated slowness. Her eyes had not left mine the entire time.

Feeling the cocktail wash imbue me once more, my heart raced, my breath shortened and I felt my groin slowly warm. She winked at me, her face turning from that of a seductress to a too young girl.

I breathed out.

The song ended and she was a tired vision once more. Stomping to the middle of the runway, she picked up a discarded bra and thong from the floor seeming more naked in only high heels. Holding her meagre coverings over herself, she hurried from the stage in a sort of belated chasteness, assiduously keeping her eyes from the audience as she left. No one seemed to notice her. To me, it seemed the spell was broken, if there was ever any magic to be found.

An equally tired looking woman stepped out into the light of the catwalk. The spell was cast again as she started her routine.

Steerforth tapped my shoulder. 'Are you coming or what?' he asked, 'You never seen tits and ass before.'

'Not so much in one night.'

I followed Steerforth to the long bar situated on the far side of the room. The bartender nodded at us and pointed at a door at the end.

'He's expecting you,' he shouted over the music, 'He's in his office.'

We passed through the doorway and up a short flight, passing a blonde on the way up. On the top of the stairwell the former spellweaver, shrugged herself into a short black cocktail dress. Neither woman acknowledged our presence. I did not seem to exist in their world – which was fine by me. My world was becoming all too crowded.

We entered the office. Behind the single desk and chair sat a sandy-haired fellow, thirtyish or so, with beagle cheeks and bloated bags under the eyes, needing a shave. He would have looked more at home propping a bar at the R.S.A. In the wrong line of business – like me.

'Ah, Brian,' Steerforth said, all humour and give, 'we've been looking for you. You remember Myers?'

Brian stood and wiped his palms down his worn grey slacks. 'Hi Steerforth,' he said looking quizzically at me. He should be wearing glasses. 'I don't think I do.'

'You remember Brian, don't you Bill?'

'No.'

'Sure you do. Carter's mate, Brian. Remember that shitty house in Arch Hill?'

'I'd remember that. I don't know any Carter.'

Steerforth was oblivious to my answer. It seems the question was disguised rhetoric. 'That was a good night,' he said, 'the old days.' There was touch of wistfulness in his manner. 'So Brian, have you got my dosh?'

Brian wiped his palms again. 'Well Alan -'

'Steerforth.'

'Steerforth...I've got ten spot at home. I'm gonna need another week for the other twenty.'

'Brian,' Steerforth said, his voice still full of good cheer, 'it was due last Friday. You know that. I'm being a generous man, but Tama he's another matter. It's business to those guys. They don't know you like I do.'

'I just need a week,' wheedled Brian, 'Can't you explain that I'm good for it?'

'Tell you what. Let's me, you and Bill here drive over to your place, get what you've got and we'll go get a drink. How does that sound? And I promise that I will speak to them about an extension.'

Brian looked doubtful.

'Don't worry so much,' said Steerforth, 'I'm a man of my word, aren't I, Bill?'

'Yeah.' A sickening pit formed in my stomach and worked its way southwards to the bowels.

'I suppose we could do that,' Brian said, 'what about this place though?'

'Shit, these places run themselves, isn't that right, Bill?'

I nodded. The need to use the toilet increased with each casual movement of my body. 'Where's your loo?'

'Down the other side of the bar,' said Brian.

'You go ahead, Bill,' Steerforth said good-humouredly, 'we'll wait for you down there. I think Brian here owes me a drink. Remember to wash your hands.'

***

Walking back down, the few girls on the stairs still did not consciously notice me. The feeling was refreshing. I was sick of being noticed and the way the evening was shaping up, I doubted that I would want to be remembered.

The toilet was where it was supposed to be. It smelt like I expected it to, sour with stale urine and old cigarettes. I stepped up to the stainless steel urinal. The bottom was littered with butts and the classic green cakes.

Unzipping my fly, the door opened once more. It was George. The stainless steel step moved beneath me as he stood beside me. As was the custom, I assiduously looked straight ahead at the wall in front of me. Someone had scrawled the word *'Cunt'* on the tiles ahead. The small lives of some were a source of fascination to me, at times.

'Your boss smiles too much,' George said.

'Hmm.' There was little to say to that remark.

'People should only smile when they are happy. He is never happy.'

'That's why I don't.' Zipping back up, I went to wash my hands in the chipped enamel basin. There was neither soap nor any thing to dry my hands on. Rinsing quickly beneath the cold water, I shook and rubbed my hands on my trousers.

As he left George said, 'Better people to be working for than him.'

Not answering, I swung back out the door. Steerforth and companion were at the bar. Brian looked uncomfortable. Steerforth had a sweaty arm around his shoulder.

'You're a popular guy.'

'Yeah, Brian,' said Steerforth, not understanding that the jibe was directed at himself, 'you're a rich man. All your mates around you.'

Brian only offered a sickly smile.

'Let's be off then,' Steerforth continued, 'Onward and Upwards, eh Bill.'

'Onwards and upwards, Steerforth. Onwards and upwards.'

As we left, I saw that another once more graced the poles. She was animated, the spell once more under evocation.

'You off, boss?' asked George as we passed him by. Brian just nodded and offered no parting comment. Steerforth kept a comradely arm around Brian as we travelled the pathway back behind the building.

The car was empty on our return. 'Where the hell has he got to?' Steerforth muttered.

'Who?' whimpered Brian.

'Me,' came Morty's voice. He emerged from the shadows of an opposite building. 'Next time park out of the light, Alan,' he said, 'too many cameras.

'Oh, shit,' whimpered Brian.

'You've met Morty, then Brian,' said Steerforth, 'I wouldn't have thought you would have had much in common. Why don't you two jump in the back and get reacquainted. Me and Bill will ride up front.'

'I don't want any trouble,' said Brian.

'Relax,' said Steerforth, 'He's just here to make sure you don't do a runner –and you're not going to be doing that. Are you?'

No reply.

'Right then,' Steerforth said. Four doors closed with a sound that would have felt at home on a prison block.

I glanced at the shining face of my watch for the first time tonight.

It was 3 a.m.

10.

The rain came down in sheets as we headed through Newmarket. Steerforth could not keep quiet. His voice chattered, increasing in pitch and volume with every passing moment. Every now and then, I detected a soft but audible whimper from the back seat. From Morty I heard nothing. With no sound to guide me, I imagined him folded away like a bat in the dark recesses, somewhere near the door handle.

We passed through Broadway, the fake façade that Newmarket had become. Driving through on the way up, I was not surprised at what it had turned to. Even all those years ago there was a hint of what this place would become. Too near the pretentious Remuera, overflowing with blue blood and social graces. Small wonder the leer of capitalism had found a place to set its lips straight on Remuera's hindquarters. Still its sight soothed my spirit, in light of Steerforth's babble.

We passed from the orange-tinted mercury lit vista into solemn darkness as we shot straight through to Manukau Road.

'Still in Hillsborough, aren't you Brian?' said Steerforth. Again the soft strangled murmur emanated from behind. 'What's the matter? Anyone would think you're being held against your will.'

'Everything will be okay, won't it Steerforth?' said Brian. His voice had become a high tenor, a strangled sob accompanied it.

'I told you. We'll get the dosh from your place and I'll talk to them. They trust me. Why don't you? Tell him Morty.'

'Everything will be fine, Brian,' Morty said.

Brian might have been satisfied with the response, but I wasn't.

'Just let me out here,' I said, 'I'll get back to Broadway and catch a cab.'

'It's pissing down out there, Bill.'

'It's alright – really.'

'No mate of mine's going to catch his death because of me,' said Steerforth. 'We'll get what owes and then we'll go out and have a good time. Isn't that right, Brian?'

'I suppose,' Brian managed.

'What about you, Morty?'

'Sounds fine, Alan. Sounds fine.'

'See Bill? It's sorted. Besides we're only ten minutes away.'

In fact, it took only five minutes. Steerforth sped down the road, gunning the European precision engine despite the weather and the greasy surfaces. We raced over a looping bridge across a section of motorway that I could not remember being there in the past. Turned at the first right, halfway up the street and we were there. The house was buried in darkness, behind a thickly forested hedge.

'You guys wait here,' said Steerforth. 'We won't be long. Will we Brian?'

'No,' said a relieved sounding Brian.

'Good. You won't have to get wet, Bill.'

Two doors – the drivers and the rear passenger side – opened and closed and two silhouettes flitted across the windscreen into the beyond. I did not hear the door to the house reciprocate, but a light from within told me that it did so.

The chill from outside had not yet dissipated – the threat of the damp still loomed near.

'Alan thinks we're a similar pair,' said Morty, 'I can't see it myself. Do you?'

'No.'

'You seem educated though.'

I shrugged. 'Unfinished English degree, years ago. I read though.'

'Ah – a man of letters. That I can appreciate. I have always had time for art. You see the world through different eyes when you have the touch of the artist about you. More like me than Steerforth, I think.'

'I'm not like anyone. My wife tells me that all the time.'

'Married then?'

'No.'

'Better off on your own. A man can realise his full potential when he roams free. I have never made any permanent connections only transient ones. That's how I got to where I am today.'

This man was not worthy of an answer.

'How long have you been working for Steerforth then?' I asked.

'I work for nobody. I'm an independent contractor.'

Between the front seats, a card appeared in the clutch of his almost fleshless hand. Reaching up to turn on the interior light, I plucked it from him, avoiding the feel of his skin. The card read: *Benjamin Mortimer. Trader.* Along with it were phone numbers – both cellular and land based – and an Epsom address.

'Trader?'

'A pretentious person might say I'm a dealer in antiques. However I'm not one of those. Though I have a philosophy against the ownership of possessions, I am not averse to feeding someone with that particular addiction.'

'Why are you here tonight then?' I asked. Maybe I had read the situation wrongly. Maybe the paranoia had set in without my sensing it. Fuck, I hoped so.

'Everyone needs a hobby,' whispered Morty. A coldness worked around my neck. 'Besides it's more profitable than the day job. Keep the card. You might want it one day. Then again – if

Steerforth's right – maybe you won't need it.' He sniggered. It sounded of scratched blackboards and sandpaper.

'Looks like tonight might be a quiet night for you then. Just a few drinks and that's it.'

'Oh I don't know about that,' said Morty.

'What do you mean?'

'I never drink and if past experience is anything to go by, I think we'll be going inside pretty shortly.'

Pulling my jacket closer around myself, I felt a shiver cut an involuntary track down my spine. This was a bloody horror movie, it had all the hallmarks – only this time the monster sounded reasonable and perverted all at once.

Morty began to whistle. It was lazy with a serpentine quality. The melody was sinuous and delving. It irritated me, but I wasn't going to tell him that. The tune was broken by a tap on my window. Peering outwards, I could see it was Brian. He gestured that we should go inside and – God help me – he was smiling.

'Told you,' said Morty.

My stomach dropped away yet again. But this time it was truly sickening. How could this man be so stupid? To be so easily deceived. Why didn't he run for his life? He must have been able to find somewhere in the darkness of suburbia.

As we got out Brian's relief is evident. 'All sorted,' he said, 'Come up. Steerforth's laying on some toot before we go.'

We traipsed up to the house. The concrete driveway was cracked and uneven, the slick texture of moss greased its surface. I slipped. My hands stopped my fall, but I felt the sting of abrasion as I hit. Tiny stones and grit pierced the soft underbelly of my hands. The damp found its way through the fabric of my trousers. Morty stooped to help me up. Fuck that – I shrugged him off.

The front door was open. We passed through. A series of photographs were arranged in geometric fashion upon the wall. A young Brian and a smiling woman, not at all attractive. Brian, slightly older and the same woman with a young girl, pretty almost angelic. They loved the camera, the camera adored them.

My churning stomach moved its way south to the bowels again.

'You have a family,' I asked rhetorically.

'No,' said Brian, 'they left me. I get to pay maintenance for the privilege though.'

The house still had an element of the feminine about it. Floral patterned curtains, a mahogany cabinet with bone china, a sense of colour coordination, but overriding it all came the feeling of gradual decline. Maybe it was the musk of fetid sock, unwashed dishes and a lack of a vacuum cleaner stroke.

Steerforth was in the living room with a phone receiver in hand. This room was a work in progress. The doorframes were only painted partially in light violet. Parts of the wallpaper had been stripped leaving the ochre tarnish of plasterboard beneath. It smelt of many night's instant dinners, cigarettes and a sour hint of exposed alcohol. Replacing the receiver back into its cradle, he spoke as Morty stepped in behind the hapless victim.

'Bit of bad news,' he said. Morty struck Brian across the back with his weapon. I knew the object. It was the long, knurled weight of the car's flashlight.' Tama accepts the conditions. You can pay us the balance in two days. But we got to take late fees out of your hide.'

There was a glint in his eyes, pure childish malevolence. He looked to Morty. 'Do him,' he said, 'nothing permanent. We want the prick to be able to walk for his money.'

Morty went about his work. He struck the sacrifice across the torso and arms. He laboured methodically and with precision. There was no emotion tied to his deed; rather it seemed to be the work of an automaton. Each blow landing exactly where it should on the target, be it rib, deltoid or scapula. It shamed me but I could detect the work of the artist here.

It showed.

All Brian did was scream. High pitched and pleading screaming, beyond the ability to formulate words and meaning.

Steerforth grabbed a cushion from the couch and stuffed it between Brian's teeth. 'Be a man,' he said, 'Bite down for the pain.' He said to Morty, 'Do an elbow. I want my money's worth.'

Morty shook his head. 'No.' He gazed at me, his eyes salamander-like and alight with predatory cunning. Then he tossed over the flashlight. 'He can do it. You I trust, Alan – I've got all the dirt I need – but you,' he said, pointing his finger at me, 'I know nothing about. So you do it. Do it right and you'll only have to do it once, you should feel it soften like a noodle beneath you.'

Looking down on the quivering mound of flesh and fabric lying on the floor like any discarded pile of refuse, I felt the shakes begin first in my toes. The feeling travelled fast through my feet to the thighs, past the pelvis, across the chest to the far reaches of fingertip and nail. Blood drained from my head. I imagined that my lips were beginning to take on the barest shade of blue.

Dropping the flashlight from my nerveless fingers, it landed heavily, echoing in the quiet house.

'Pick it up,' said Morty.

'No.'

'If you don't, you'll be down there with him. Except you won't be getting back up.'

'Come on, Bill,' said Steerforth, 'it's just business.'

'Yeah – come on, Bill,' whispered Morty.

I stooped and retrieved the weapon. It felt dead in my hands – as nerveless as my fingers. I looked back down at that mess that was Brian.

'I'll help you,' said Morty. He reached down and grabbed Brian's arm, twisting it to expose a pointed elbow. Brian squealed and begged. He could only say one word.

'Please,' he squealed, 'please.'

'Shut up,' I heard myself say, 'Shut the fuck up.' My voice seemed to have increased an octave. Brian couldn't hear. He couldn't do anything but mouth the same word into the carpet. 'Shut up,' I screamed. Raising the flashlight high above the shoulder, I brought it down. It missed the elbow, instead hitting the upper arm. Raising it again, I dropped it with full force and connected with the target. I actually heard the crack of the joint as it broke at its natural fulcrum. Morty was right. The arm took on a squishy quality; it could be felt from the other end of the bludgeon.

Brian screamed.

'Shut up.' I kicked Brian hard and fast. 'Shut up. Shut up.' Who pulled me off? I didn't know whether it was Morty or Steerforth. Shit, I didn't remember stopping.

'Shut up.' It had become a mantra, a form of security.

'Christ, Bill,' Steerforth said, 'you only had to do the elbow. No need for that.'

'Shut up.'

Steerforth bent and picked Brian up by the hair. 'You've got two days. You come to me. Don't make me look for you.'

'Fuck you,' said Brian. He spat a heavy bloody gobbet of phlegm onto the threadbare carpet. Waves of golden respect emanated from me to land on Brian's beat-up carcass.

Steerforth rammed the head into the floor. Once. Twice. 'No. Fuck you, Brian.' He lets the head drop and as an afterthought lands a kick into the body. 'Let's go,' he said.

A hand came to rest on my shoulder. I turned to see Morty smiling at me with a paternalistic maw, the proud face of a father. 'You did all right Bill. Can I call you, Bill?' He extended his hand down and clasped my own – it felt cold and dry. 'You can call me, Morty. You've earned the right to.'

Looking back, with what I am sure is a blank face, my stomach churned, the blood had not returned to my head. I knew what followed this feeling.

It did not take long to rush outside – quicker than it took to come in. I emptied the contents of my stomach out onto the broken concrete slabs of the driveway. Retches came in jarring bursts, bruising the insides, the ribs crackled and popped under the strain, the sternum begged me to cease.

The slap of a palm cracked across my shoulder blades. The jovial cackle of Steerforth seeped into my eardrums. 'Just think of it as training,' he said, 'you'll be in shape in no time.'

'You'll do okay,' said Morty, 'It just takes practice.'

Not looking at them, I staggered to the car and got in the passenger side not sure if I slammed the door or not. I fucking slammed it in my mind though.

'So what about that drink then?' said Steerforth as he gets in the driver's side, 'I asked Brian, but he didn't seem up to it. Soft cock.'

'Just take me back,' I said resigned.

'We'll just have a quick one.'

'No.'

'You can get me home too,' said Morty, 'I'm not being paid to socialise.'

'Fucking ingrates,' says Steerforth. He turned the key and planted the car into reverse. At the bottom of the drive we heard and felt the harsh metallic scrape of contact. Letterbox versus BMW. A cool draw.

'Shit,' said Steerforth and climbed out to inspect the damage. Morty exited to join him. Remaining seated, I was consciously oblivious to what was happening. They became bodiless voices: distant and ethereal.

'Fuck it.'

'It's just a bit of paint.'

'You don't have to bloody well pay for it.'

'No I don't, Alan.'

The car doors slammed again. My gaze had not erred from staring straight out the windscreen.

'You got nothing to say?' said Steerforth. No answer from this quarter. 'Right then.'

We sped off into the night.

'Don't go too fast, Alan,' said Morty, 'we don't want to be stopped.'

Steerforth made inaudible mutterings beneath his breath.

'What was that, Alan?' asked Morty.

No reply.

I did not notice the drive back to Morty's rundown house. I did not notice the city, remember how it was back in some far off day. The way the light reflected off the rain-swept streets, did not capture my attention. All I could see was a bruised and bloody Brian mouthing 'Please' into a dirty carpet.

We parked in that Kingsland street and Steerforth and Morty voiced pleasantries as if they existed in a civilised world.

'Get in touch if you need me Friday, Alan.'

'Will do, Morty.'

A hand passed over from the backseat.

'Nice to meet you, Bill. You will get used to it. You're a natural'

Bugger shaking his hand. I just continued staring straight ahead. The hand retreated.

'Be seeing you, Alan.'

'Yeah, see you Morty.

The rear door closed and I watched the skeletal man return to his lair. Gazed as the broken door swallowed him up in one ravenous bite. My shoulders slumped, a long slow breath escaped, the taste of bile burned.

'You wouldn't believe the amount of cash that man has secreted away in that place,' murmured Steerforth, 'If he didn't scare me shitless, I'd fucking take it.'

Saying nothing in return, I fixed my stare back out at some point beyond the windscreen.

'Fuck, you even whine when you're saying nothing,' said Steerforth.

We drove back to Sandringham Road. Steerforth tossed three one hundred dollar bills into my lap in the parking lot.

'Money is not always this easy to come by, Bill.'

I just got out and walked to the front doors of my new home. Daylight was just starting to show its face. I scaled the long staircase to my room, flopped on top of the bed. Staring at the textured ceiling I did not notice when the sleep took hold of me.

11.

'I'm the best dressed scarecrow in town,' I said to the mirror.

Buttoning the jacket closed, I turned a brief profile to both sides. It was a nice cut. Even off this rapidly declining frame the suit sat reasonably well. A pity about the head that popped out the collar, the hair in chaotic disarray: jumbled and lank, the widow's peak even more pronounced.

The brown loafers that stuck out the ends of the trouser legs did not go well with the ensemble either. They were stained by the previous night's rain. I still wore the mustard rayon shirt. The colour matched, but I could smell the brackish odour of sweat and cigarettes wafting from the armpits, seeping from beneath the jacket.

I shuddered, as much at the distorted memory of past events as to the smells that turned my gut queasy.

The face in the mirror stared back. The webs of lines that stretched from the corners of the eyes seem more deeply ingrained into the flesh. The bags beneath the bottom lids were definitely darker, had a more bruised appearance. My face had an ashen complexion; a slightly jaundiced pallor dusted the cheeks. Sticking out my tongue, I saw it was white with a furry texture. It looked like it tasted. I looked like how I felt: hungover, troubled and old.

'How's it looking in there?' Sam called from beyond the door.

'The suit is great,' I said, 'the rest...I don't know.' I walked out into the shop.

'It hangs well off you,' Sam said.

'That's what I thought.'

Sam turned to the shop assistant who looked dapper when compared to me.

'What do you think, Carl?' Sam asked.

'It looks fine. He'll need different shoes and as for that shirt...' He wrinkled his delicate nose.

'Carl?' I asked.

'Oh, I'm sorry. I forgot to introduce you two. Bill, Carl. Carl, Bill.'

Conscious of my alcohol breath and vile armpits, I tried to infuse an element of friendliness in my smile. Carl must have misread the attempt. A frown momentarily flickered across his features to be replaced by cool neutrality.

'Hello,' he said, 'Now we must find you some shirts. The good thing about a basic black suit is that you can alter your entire appearance with a good shirt.' He scuttled to a shelf and picked off three cellophane packaged shirts, a red, a pale blue and a light violet shade. 'I'm guessing your neck size but I think I'm right.' He looked back at Sam. 'What time do you start tonight?'

'Nine o'clock. I thought we'd eat out.'

'Ok, I'll try to be back by six. For God's sake, get that man some shoes as well.'

Sam looked at me uncertainly for a minute and then kissed Carl. 'I'll see you tonight. We'll go to *Italia* I think.'

'Make it *Georgio's*. The fettuccini was horrible last time.'

Outside on Broadway, Sam confided in me. 'I know he seems much younger, but there's only five years difference.'

'No business of mine.' A cold sweat had worked its way from my brow-line downwards. My stomach was playing hopscotch with my intestines.

'I know,' said Sam, 'but it's what everyone thinks.'

'I'm not thinking anything. I feel too horrible.'

'Oh,' said Sam, looking slightly miffed, 'there's a shoe place down there and then we'll get that breakfast I promised you. I've got something to show you.'

***

We sat in the car afterwards – me loaded down with bags of clothes and shoes on my lap, feeling like an ill-dressed poodle. I turned to Sam. 'Why couldn't we have eaten in Newmarket?'

'I told you,' said Sam, a slight smile played across his well-fed face, 'I've got something to show you.'

The car headed up Khyber Pass and down Symonds Street towards the CBD. Parking just below Albert Park in a multi-layered car park, Sam chose a space on the ground floor near the exits.

'Where exactly are we going?' I said, as I slammed my door shut. My head was pounding now, the brain shrunken and twisted. No type of food and coffee would make me feel any better. The cold sweat continued its steady drip from my forehead.

'You're going to wreck the surprise,' Sam said, 'it's not far.'

Wandering down to High Street, each step I took seemed to be one further into a sickly oblivion. I struggled to keep up with Sam who walked with a pace that was just beyond the scope of my ability.

Eventually we stopped in front of a narrow café. It seemed to me that this place had sat for so long between the outer buildings that it had given up the ghost about living and had instead opted to shrivel up and slowly succumb to the weight of its long standing neighbours. Two small tables with marine-coloured umbrella stands speared through the middle, sat gaily on the pavement, surrounded by shining chrome chairs. The sign on the thin window announced this establishment as *Alginon* in fine gold painted script. Below the signage, a flyer had been stuck to the glass. It warned of something called *Y2K*. What the fuck was that?

We walked inside and a long counter rode along the exposed brick internal wall. Smells of food being prepared assailed my nose. My stomach groaned. I was sick of my stomach's complaints.

'Sammy,' said the counterman with an indeterminate European accent, 'Long time, no see.'

'Hi, Gregory,' said Sam, 'it's only been a week.'

'That's a long time in this business.'

'Tell me about it. When do you leave?'

'As soon as I get rid of this place. No interest. They all want it for a song. It's High Street for God's sake. I won't sell it for less than it is worth. I won't.' His voice increased in emotion as he spoke.

'I'm sure something will turn up,' Sam said.

The conversation blurred into meaningless noise. I looked around. The café was understated in a good way. There were punters sitting at the counter, or in conversation at the tables that lined the other wall. It was a good class of clientele as well. They all seemed professional, with time on their hands and credit on their cards. It had a certain character to it that was neither pretentious, nor too colloquial. If I had been in a better frame of mind I am sure I would have warmed to this place.

As it was, it was all I could do to keep my hands from shaking. My attention turned back to the conversation.

'What can we get for you today, my friend,' said Gregory.

'Eggs Benedict,' said Sam, 'for me and my pal here. And two long blacks.'

'Where will you be sitting?'

'Outside,' I interjected, 'I need to smoke.' Not for the first time I cursed the politically correct, healthy gods that reigned at the end of twentieth century New Zealand. As always I vented my condemnation in silence.

We took a number and sat at an umbrella-festooned perch. Shaking a cigarette loose hurriedly from a packet, I lit and dragged on it deep. A cough from my gut erupted violently. It continued aggressively for what seemed like long moments.

'You want to give those things up, bro' Sam said. 'They sound like they're killing you.'

I shrugged noncommittally.

Our coffees were brought out to us. The bitter taste of grounds and water made the cigarette bearable to puff upon. The acidic tasting juice however, did nothing to alleviate the state of my wellbeing, but on the bright side it did not make me feel any worse.

Breakfast arrived. It looked sumptuous and tasty. However, this did nothing to make it any more appetising. I tentatively cut into a portion of bagel, egg and hollandaise sauce and spooned it onto my tongue. The creamy richness of the hollandaise caused my stomach to rebel, returning the fork -still dripping- to the edge of the plate. I said, 'I can't eat this.'

'Just get through it,' Sam said, 'You'll feel better for it. I promise.'

Breathing deep, I picked up the cutlery once more and returned to the task at hand. A few bites later and the eggs took on a bearable quality, halfway through and there was some semblance of enjoyment in the undertaking. We ate in silence: Sam in pure enjoyment and me less so.

'So what do you think?' Sam said, as the plates are cleared away.

'You're right. I do feel a bit better.'

'No, I mean about this place.'

'It's alright, I guess.'

Sam leaned forward across the table, his voice lowered. 'I'm going to buy it. Gregory is going to become desperate to move soon. Then I'm going to make him an offer just over what he already has. He'll take it and be grateful and I'll have a bargain café.'

'Why?'

Sam sighed. 'If I'm lucky I get to see Carl a couple of hours a day. I'm going to lose him if I don't change something. Too many good looking men in this town.'

'You two seem happy together.'

'There's been a bit of distance lately. I can't fix it the way we are. So...' He waved his hands in the general direction of the café. 'How do you feel about running it,' he asked.

'What about Steerforth?'

'What about the prick? I don't owe him a thing. I've helped him out enough. Shit, I introduced him to people when he didn't have a bean and now he resents it.'

'Who, Morty?' A shudder ran through me involuntarily.

'Who? No, some of my extended whanau. Bad pricks. He wanted to play with the big boys but they're sucking him up now. I'm not going to be there when it happens and neither should you. Shit sticks.'

I stay silent and look for another cigarette.

'Well, think about it,' Sam said, 'you handled Steerforth last night. I'm grateful for that. I like you.'

'You don't know me.'

Finding another cigarette, I lit it, puffed at it then stubbed it out in the ashtray. 'Is the art gallery still down the road?'

'Yeah. Don't you think you should get some sleep before tonight? It's your first full night.'

'I'll make it. You go on ahead. I'll get a bus.'

***

I wandered down the narrow vista that was High Street, bags of clothes in hand, my head still thick. The city by day seemed a different beast to that of its nightly incarnation. It was all business fronts, shining glass and bustle. Mothers with children in tow walked next to latte carrying professionals and urbanite do-nothings. There was none of the sleaziness of the upper city here, that characterisation seemed to have been washed away by a wave of new culture. I was unsure whether that manifestation was good or bad. It was not a hateful vision, like the sight of Newmarket.

As I spot the white stone shell of the gallery, I gazed upon the oasis that was Albert Park above. That's what made this area palatable. Patches of a natural world still existed. It was not all concrete trappings. But for how long, I wondered.

My reverie was halted by a sight that I did not expect to see. Ahead of me on the other side, a figure stood closely inspecting the contents of a shop display. It couldn't be. I stopped and ducked into a doorway.

She was dressed differently. A shapeless black peasant skirt, ballooned from her hips and a simple green top accentuated her thinness. But I recognised her more from her demeanour than by her appearance.

Jasmine. She peered intently at something beyond the store window. Her gaze seemed to drill a hole through the melted silica into the void beyond.

Pale by day, she seemed to belong to this place as much as I did – not at all. I felt intrusive from my hiding place. A part of the dirty raincoat brigade. The shopping bags seemed to weigh heavier at the end of my arms. Gripping them tighter, I forgot my position and peered closer at the washed-out vision across the street.

'Can I help you, sir?'

It was an elegantly dressed man – middle aged, everything about him shouted prim. His lips were pursed as if I was trespassing on some unseen domain.

'I'm just looking, thanks.'

'In this store, sir?'

I looked back through the window. She was not there.

'What exactly are you looking for?'

'It doesn't matter.' Pushing past the assistant, I clambered out into the street and looked back up towards the gallery. No sign of her. Glimpsing a hint of green and black making its way back down towards Downtown, in the other direction, I followed in a half-run. The shopping bags gathered around my legs, impeding my motion forward. I stumbled and then righted myself.

Gaining some ground, her form loomed larger in front of me. Holding back slightly, I walked at a consistent pace behind her, keeping a few pedestrians between her and me.

I tripped on one of the bags. It dropped to the ground. A box containing glossy, black Italian leather shoes spilled forth. Scrambling on the ground, I managed to gather it all back and stand.

She was gone – couldn't be far. I scuttled forwards, cheeks slightly reddened by this unseemly public debacle. Everyone was probably looking at me. Never had been one to call attention to myself. When it happened I preferred to drop from sight and just negate my presence from all in sundry.

Couldn't do that here. Firstly, I was in a busy narrow street with no immediate routes for escape. Secondly, she would get away if I was too subtle.

Moving faster, I looked into the shop fronts for a sign of her. At first I picked every window, peered through each window past the signage for a glimpse of her. A tobacconist, a designer clothes shop, a camera stop, a designer clothes shop, a shoe store, a designer clothes shop, a picture framers.

In time, I became more selective, choosing the stores that might interest someone like her. But what was someone like her? I didn't know before. Fucked if I knew now. All the while, I looked further down the street.

Now it was a designer clothes façade, a select bookstore, a shop specialising in ceramic pottery at exorbitant prices. I realised I had picked up the pace, moving at a slow trot. My breath had become ragged. I was a man that smoked too many cigarettes, aware that I stood out in this crowd. A scruffy middle-aged man in a stinking suit, hair awry, vein-shot eyes, panting, probably slightly crazed looking, sweating alcohol fumes, with fucking shopping bags.

She had disappeared, flitted away in the sunlight, a daytime phantom, possibly a figment of some ensuing dementia. I was directly across from *Alginon*. My exertion had bought me full circle, ending at the beginning.

I sighed and wandered back through its narrow doors. Gregory looked up. He threw me a nod.

'Long black, right.'

'Yeah.'

Sitting once more at the same table, I shook yet another cigarette loose from the diminishing packet. Fuck it, I would splash out on a taxi. Didn't have a clue where to pick a bus up from anyway. My coffee was brought to me. I took a long deep gut drag from my smoke and blew it out to join the exhaust fumes.

'Why were you following me?' her voice rolled over my shoulder.

I didn't feel the shock of being revealed. I was too tired. Age pushed two heavy hands down onto my shoulders. Without turning around, I said, 'I just wanted to know. That's all.' I dragged deep, exhaled and took the rest of his coffee in one long gulp and turned.

She had gone.

I found a cab. The burden of weariness took me on the journey and I dropped from consciousness. It required the irritated shake of a taxi driver to bring me around again.

Inside my room, I dropped to the bed and slept once more.

12.

'Who's the pretty boy then?'

My cheeks reddened. 'It's for the job. I gotta look the part.'

'If you want to do that, at least have a shave.' The palm of her hand cut a path down my cheek. 'You've let yourself go. I remember when you used to make an effort for me.'

'I've been busy getting things sorted.'

'How's that? Drinking with the boys? Out on the town with that prick? I think you're losing your resolve.'

'How am I going to do anything without getting close to him? Do you think I'm enjoying this? Fuck's sake, it's all I can do to keep it together.'

'I don't know what you think. That's always the problem with you – bottling everything inside. For all I know, you resent me for this. Planning to get rid of me. Shit, you smell like a fucking brewery.'

'Everything I've ever done has been for you. You damn well know that. Christ do you think I like this? I had to beat someone I didn't even know. It's going to haunt me...it haunts me now. I'm not this person. It's all for you.'

'If that's the way you feel, I'll leave.'

'Maybe you should.'

'You'd like that wouldn't you.'

'Oh for fuck's sake...'

13.

'Where are we going?' asked Morgana.

'The *Hyperium*.'

'Good. Someone with money probably. If I'm lucky they'll extend for a few hours.'

I didn't reply. The sleep had washed away my age somewhat. Sitting in the driver's seat of a car that smacked of quality, my suit and new shoes upon me, I felt elegant. My appearance had thrown a cloak of confidence across my shoulders. I sat straight in my seat, my hands gripped the steering wheel with a poise that I hadn't felt in years. I was a brave new man plotting an assured course.

'My name's not Morgana, you know?' she said. Her raven hair blended with the dimness of the interior light. All I could determine was the chalky complexion of her face, the movement of her darkly painted lips. She had chosen a long flowing evening dress, a dark crimson, low cut, accentuating her breasts. Encircling her neck was a choker collar with a cameo at its centre.

'I know.'

'Don't you want to know what it really is?'

'Not really. One names as good as another.'

She chuckled. 'You really know how to make a girl feel good about herself. You're a strange man.'

'I've been told that before.'

'By who?'

'Someone in another life.'

She shrugged. 'That's ok. Everyone's got to have his or her secrets. Makes life interesting.'

I felt comfortable.

'It's Susan,' she said.

'What?'

'My name. It's Susan. A shit name for a whore. Doesn't fit with the whole illusion. So I'm Morgana. I even use the name off the job now. It's sort of cool, don't you think?'

'It suits you.'

She smiled. 'Why I do believe you're paying me a compliment.'

'Maybe.'

She stretched out luxuriantly in her seat and let out a yawn. 'I hope it's an Asian businessman,' she said, 'Lots of money to spend and hopefully a small cock. Probably come quick too.' She looked at me. 'Oh, sorry.'

'What about?'

'You know, last time we hooked up.'

'I don't really remember,' I lied, 'I had a good time.'

'You're sweet.' It amazed me how women could turn a term of endearment. Twist it like putty into a completely different meaning. Yet at face value, they could say what they meant. Take this instance. At the surface level she probably did mean what she said. But she also was using those two words as a form of apology, ingraining it with a slice of pity. She had made three complete statements from just two words. In women, I found the talent desirable. It gave them an air of mystique, that unattainable something that I would never understand yet would always enjoy trying to find out.

I realised for the first time since I left Levin, I was actually enjoying myself in someone's company. There was nothing too personal, no ulterior motivations other than conversation. It was friendship without being friends, enjoyment without real cost. It was easy.

The car crawled its way down between the ever-changing stops and starts of the Queen Street traffic lights.

'Did you know you were my first?' I asked.

'You're not telling me you were a virgin.'

'In a way. I haven't slept with anyone other than my wife in the last fifteen years. So in a way I was sort of a born again virgin.'

'You didn't sleep with me. You fucked me.'

'Yeah, but you know what I mean.'

'You've got to make the distinction. Us girls, we're whores, prostitutes whatever you want to call us. I fuck men for money. That's it. When I started out, I had men friends who I could say I slept with. But I'm too tired to deal with that shit now. So now I fuck for money and take my sleep when I can get it.'

'I get it.'

'Make sure you do. You don't want to get hurt.'

We pulled into the semi-circular entranceway of the *Hyperium*. It was the fast-becoming grand old dame of hotels. It stretched upwards looking down to the Hauraki Gulf.

'Where do I park?'

'You don't have to. I'll just get out here.'

'Don't I have to check it out – get the money?'

'No, hotel gigs are usually pretty safe. I'll meet you in the lobby later.' She took a breath and threw me a brief smile. 'I get stage fright – even now.' Morgana closed the door behind her and made her way to the lobby. A uniformed doorman followed her progress, watching the lithe sway of her hips. The scarlet number she had on accentuated her curves. She looked sexier now than what I remembered of her naked and on top of me. There was mystery about the provocatively dressed woman. Especially when it was done with a sense of elegance. Trashy mini-skirts and come-fuck-me boots screamed sex, but to me it was too brash. That mode did not stimulate the imagination the way Morgana did.

Maybe sensuality was all to do with the packaging. The thought disturbed me.

Flipping open the phone, I called Sam. 'I've dropped her off. What now.'

'Pick up Steerforth at his place. He's got a job for you.'

'What sort of job?' A flashing image of Brian screaming into a carpet flashed across my mind.

'I don't know. You know him better than I do.'

'Where does he live?'

'You don't know? Grey Lynn. One of those new shitty apartments. Hold on I'll get an address.' He told me. I knew where Grey Lynn was but not the street.

'Map book is in the glove box, Bill. Hurry, time is money.'

Opening the glove box, I pulled out the book and traced my finger across the appropriate map under the dim glow of the interior light. I found it.

A car horn shrieked behind me. I heard a faint voice. 'Get a fucking move on.'

The doorman tapped on my window, 'You'll have to move, sir,' he called through the glass. I waved to him, threw the car into gear and stalled, turned the ignition, made a silent plea to the gods that it wouldn't be flooded, started the car and set off into the youthful night.

***

Steerforth was waiting for me kerbside outside a cubic, uninteresting apartment block. 'What took you so long,' he complained.

'I had to find my way from the *Hyperium*. It all seems different around here now.'

Steerforth sniffed. 'I hadn't noticed.'

'Where to?'

'Glen Innes,' he said. 'Got to drop that cash.'

I reached for the map. 'You won't need that,' Steerforth said, 'Just get on the motorway. I'll show you where.'

The rain began to drop once more. I was sure that Auckland never rained this much years ago. Sure it rained, but now its flavour was more tropical. Just descended without warning onto the unsuspecting heads below. Memory had that effect though. Perhaps it had always been like this. Maybe it was all a wistful remembrance of a world that had never existed. I wasn't sure.

We took the Mt Wellington turnoff, down the Panmure highway and crossed the boundary into Glen Innes. It was really only a wall of industrialised buildings, factories, warehouses and workshops and a rusting Morris 8 stuck on a pole on top of a wrecker's yard that demarcated the line between Panmure and Glen Innes. The houses on either side of the border were the same. Rows of plain semi-detached state housing, rusting car hulks, grass verges left unattended by the city councils on the poorly lit streets. There was a sameness about each street. A uniformity inspired by bored government planners in far off offices.

I turned into a darkened side road, outside a high corrugated iron fence. The fences to the left and right of the property had all been tagged in strange monikers. This fence however remained untouched, not clean but not splashed in graffiti either.

'Come on then,' said Steerforth.

'You want me to go in as well.'

'See that,' he said. He points to two faint red lights at either end of the fence-line. 'Cameras. If

I go in there without you, they'll only wonder why.'

We got out and crossed to the gate. Steerforth pressed the button on a crudely fixed intercom system.

'Yeah?' A bored voice crackled through the static from the other side. There was a hint of music in the background. Hip hop noise.

'It's Steerforth.'

'What do you want?'

'Do you really want to do this out on the road?'

'Wait a minute.'

It took five. Finally the gates opened inwards. They squealed on their hinges, the bottom scraped on the driveway. Inside a monster greeted us. He was huge, dressed in dirty jeans, a t-shirt topped off in a dirty leather jacket. A moko was ingrained in blue ink from his eyes downward. His lips were stained deep blue by the tattooist's gun.

'How is it?' Steerforth said, 'Tama around?'

The biker didn't answer, just turned and stomped back to the house. If you could call it that.

Although it was a standard three-bedroom weatherboard house, it had more the look of a fortress about it. Two Harleys parked haphazardly on the outside gleamed darkly in the house lights. Their motors tinkled: hot metal reacting to the cold of the night. Another leather clad member stood at the front door, smaller in stature than his compatriot but still large and no less menacing, wearing a beard that ran over his chest.

As we drew closer, I heard a rush of movement and a frenzied snarl. I jumped sideward, colliding with Steerforth. A dog: knee high and bull-headed strained at the end of a thickly linked chain. The man at the door sniggered. 'What the fuck are we doing here?' I whispered.

'Just keep your mouth shut and follow me,' hissed Steerforth, 'Don't be a smart ass.'

We moved on up two short, concrete steps to the door. The beast that waited there, stared deeply into my eyes, probing me. It seemed to me that he didn't like what he found there. I felt a tremble work its way through my body. I swallowed and looked down.

'Who the fuck is this,' he said to Steerforth.

'My driver. He's cool.'

'Fucking tell us who you're bringing next time.'

'Yeah, sorry.'

We walked through to the living room – if that is what you could call it. On the wall a giant flag sits depicted the caricature of a tusked boar: snarling and menacing, dark blood running from its mouth. Emblazoned in black letters around it was the title, *CUTTERS M.C.*

A cheap knocked-up bar had been erected in the corner. The only furniture consisted of an expensive leather couch and a pool table. Two of the Cutters played at it. Another -the largest of all- was behind the bar counter. He had Cutters tattooed across the breadth of his neck in heavy Germanic script. A large boar, the twin of the one displayed on the wall, was inked onto his cheek.

The music in here was loud. Lots of 'bitches' and 'muthafuckers'. It seemed an appropriate form for the environment.

'Is he out the back?' Steerforth asked the bearded one. He received a curt nod in return. 'I'll just go out then.' He turned to me, his face neutral and hard. 'Wait here. I won't be long.'

'What?'

'Relax. I won't be long.'

I felt anything but relaxed. The attitude in the room was ominous. I looked over at the Cutter behind the makeshift bar. The Cutter looked back and blew me a leering kiss. Jesus, what had I got myself into? The two at the pool table stopped their game and looked me up and down. Only an hour before I had felt confident in my new clothes. One could have described my appearance as suave, now I felt overdone.

Steerforth left the room, a Cutter in tow. I had never wanted anyone to stay with me so bad since I was a child. Even then I don't think the want was as intense. The eyes around the room had not left me.

'Nice threads, bro,' said the tattooed henchman in the corner.

'Thanks.'

'Have a beer.'

'No, thanks.'

'Our beer not good enough, bro?'

I looked up and found myself being looked directly in the eye. It was not quite threatening, more an appraising stare – but who could really tell. A cold thrill danced upon me. My bladder felt full and my insides were looser. 'It's not that. I just -'

'Then have one.' A leather clad arm reached into a battered, peeling fridge, withdraws a large brown bottle. Blue inked fingers extracted a lighter from a pocket and expertly popped the lid. The bottle was slammed down onto the chipped bar top.

Grabbing at it, I took a long deep swig, making certain I didn't grimace at the bitter taste and returned the bottle to the surface.

An arm snaked over my shoulder. The hand that connected to it had a large two-paper joint burning between the fingers. I had not heard them come up behind me.

'Toke?' Sour breath combined with the sweetness of the herb. I took it, sucked back a big hit and tried to hand it back.

'Have another. We got plenty.'

Expelling the smoke from my lungs, I took another toke. This time the hand accepted the joint back. The arm belonged to a body, but I didn't want to see which body it belonged to.

'Nice shoes, bro,' the voice connected to the joint continued. 'If you weren't so small I'd have to take them off you.'

The Cutters all laughed. I was a small man in a world of giants. Sweating freely, I realised I had never felt true fear. But I felt it now. I could not escape if I chose to, I would be cut down before I made it to the door. They would have lived up to their name.

My phone both vibrated and rung in my pocket. I ignored it.

'You not going to answer that, bro?'

I shook my head slightly. 'No, I'll get it later.'

'Someone you don't want us to hear. You're not a pig are you?'

'No.'

'You sure, bro? Let's empty your pockets and find out, eh.'

'Look it'll be my boss. He'll want me to pick someone up or drop them off. It's nothing.' The fear reached the apex of its proportions now. I needed to shit desperately – could feel a hysterical laugh working its way up my throat.

'So how is my cousin?' The new voice came from behind me, from the doorway.

Turning to the voice, I recognised him from last night. It was small Sam, the figure from the office doorway. His arm sat around a woman: twentyish, Maori and proud looking.

This man was different from the rest. He looked just as menacing. A shaved head, the dome inked in tribal designs. But he was smaller than the others. Dressed differently as well. Not overly flash -a collared linen shirt, black jeans and a leather waistcoat- but definitely a cut above his friends. A dangerous vision.

'He's okay,' I said.

'You're a man that keeps his eyes open. That's a useful thing.'

'Thanks.'

'He's a good man is Sam. Even if he isn't one of us.'

'I like him.'

'What's your name?'

'Bill.'

'How do you like your mate, Steerforth?'

I shrugged. 'He's my boss.'

'Not like Sam though is he?'

'No.'

'If you have any problems with him, come see me. Anytime. Tell the prick Tama says he's got until Friday.'

'Yeah. Where is he?'

'He left you here, bro. Hope your car is still there.'

'I've got the keys. I gotta go.' I looked to Tama to see if this was okay and felt the presence of the others behind him, looming hulks of humanity.

Tama's girl sensed my discomfort and laughed.

'That boy looks like he's gonna wet himself,' she said. She didn't know how on the money she was.

Tama stepped away to leave the door clear. 'Remember call me. Say gidday to Sam for me.'

I nodded, pushed past and stepped out the front door. The Harleys looked even more menacing than before. I was expecting the dog this time but it made no move towards me, just let out a low growl. Pulling at the gate, I expected the car to be somehow gone.

Steerforth was waiting on the kerb. 'Took your time,' he said.

'You left me in there.'

'He told me to leave by the back.'

'I don't ever want to go there again.'

Steerforth waved his hand at me. 'Relax, you'll get used to it. You're one of us. Come on, drop us off. You got to be out there making me money.'

'Fuck off. I'm just the driver. Remember?'

My phone set my pocket alight once more.

'Where were you,' Sam said.

'G.I with the boss.'

'You meet my cousin?'

'Yeah.'

'Don't get too chummy with him. He'll suck you dry.'

'No kidding.'

'Right. When you're done, back to the *Sheraton*.'

I snapped back the receiver. 'Right,' I said. 'Let's do this job.'

14.

'What a cheap prick,' Morgana said. She handed the money over. 'Didn't want to use a condom, then when I said that it wasn't an option, he wanted to do it at discount. Arsehole.'

'But you got all the money.'

'Damn straight, I did. I am an expensive girl with expensive tastes. If I wanted to do it cheap, I'd work the streets and freeze my arse off. Fuck that.'

'You've got another job,' I said. 'In Greenlane. A motel.'

'Good. It's better out here than back at the parlour.' She reached into her purse and drew out a cigarette. 'For one thing I can smoke. They won't let you do it back there. Doesn't look classy enough. Haven't they ever looked at old movies? Women looked chic with a cigarette in their mouth. It's almost a phallic thing, the subconscious blowjob, should encourage clients to spend money. Not there though...or any parlour I've worked at. Cretins.'

'You sound like Sam. You must have a business brain.'

'Sam's okay. He's the reason I work where I do. As long as you do the job, he sorts the money for you. Always on time and up front. You've seen that photo in his room?'

'Rita Hayworth?'

She nodded. 'It's a still from *Gilda.* Not a poster shot... an actual still. Anyone who loves Rita that much is all right in my book. Of course he says he likes it because he sees it as the ultimate gay love story. But doesn't he have a picture of Glenn Ford and George Macready. Why have the jilted other? I reckoned it is because he's a sucker for the working girl. Likes style as well. That's why I like him. I trust him because of it. What about you?'

'I like some old movies. Couldn't tell you the actors though. I'm more of a reader really.'

'What about the style in those days? Doesn't it grab you?'

'I don't know. I just liked the stories.'

She shook her head and snorted. 'Fucking men.'

The roads were quieter. It was a middling time, a low point; traffic was scarcer as we travelled the Great South Road. The streetlights cast a line of fluctuating shadow across Morgana's face as we headed towards the start of suburbia. The boundary by which urban met suburban was marked by a string of motels. I pulled in halfway down. It was a 'U' shaped two-storey affair, no lights on in the office, '*No Vacancy*' flashed on the sign out front.

'It's Unit 3 according to Sam,' I said.

'You can check this one out for me. It's sort of dark around here. Too many shadows. I don't like the dark.'

It was a ground floor unit. An outside light threw a beam over the tarnished brass door number. I could hear the sound of a television inside – determined the sound of guns. Must have been a war movie or a cop show. I knocked on the eggshell coloured door. No reply, knocked again. As I turned to leave it opened. A heavy smell of ganja wafted out to greet my nostrils. Along with the smell a figure appeared.

He was youngish – twenties or so – red-eyed and had a stupid smile plastered across his mush.

'Hi,' I said. 'You ordered some company this evening?'

It took a while for the boy/man to answer. 'Ah – yeah. How much is it?' He looked sheepish. 'I haven't done this before.'

'It's two eighty, mate.' I found the negotiation nerve-wracking even though I was the one in control. 'I'll take that now and I'll go get the lady.'

'Is she a looker? I'm not shelling out for a dog.'

A wave of disgust rose to the fore. 'I think Morgana will meet your requirements, sir,' I said, 'maybe even surpass them.'

I know I should have winked knowingly at him or maybe thrown some sort of leer onto my face. Bad movies and cheap books dictated this fact. But I wasn't going to. I might have been in a cheap job, but that was fit for a purpose. I'd fucked if I would cheapen myself in the process.

Thus ended the resolution for the day.

'Is there anyone in there with you?' I asked.

A brief flicker of uncertainty crossed the punter's features. 'No,' he said. 'Why would there be?'

'Just checking,' I said. 'We want to keep everyone safe and above board, don't we?'

I was nervous. Something was not quite right. It was just a feeling, but these types of feelings had held true in the past. 'Do you mind if I have a look around. Just to make sure,' I said.

The punter showed a wide expansive arm, inviting me inside. 'Help yourself,' he said. 'No one home.'

I popped my head inside the doorway. It was open plan, beige and tasteless. A sparse lounge opened up into a kitchenette. A television blared opposite a sofa and two semi-comfortable looking kitsch armchairs. On the wall facing him there was a still life – a floral arrangement in a jar. How original. There was a closed door on one side.

'That the bedroom? I'll take a quick peek in there if you don't mind.'

He sighed and stomped over to the offending entrance and flung the door open. No one was inside the equally boring bedroom with the olive covered queen-sized bed and another original still life. 'Satisfied?' he said.

'Perfectly. Now all I need is the dosh and I'll bring her up.'

He reached into the pocket of his chemically faded jeans and pulled out a battered leather wallet. 'How about a discount for cash?' he said.

'No, mate. We're not a charitable institution. If you don't want the service, I'll fuck off now,' I said, letting my irritation ride into my tone.

'No that's alright,' he said. 'You just gotta try these things.' He counted out the faded green twenty-dollar notes. Each of them looked like they had spent time in a trouser pocket within the throes of a spin cycle.

'Fine, I'll go get her.' I was still uneasy. It played out in my furtive steps, as I walked back to the car and got in the driver's side.

'I don't know about this one,' I said to Morgana. 'Something's a bit off.'

'It'll be fine. He looks like a pussy cat,' she said. "You should see some of the monsters I've fucked.'

'It's not how he looks. It's just a vibe I'm getting. He's up to something.'

'He's probably just shitting his pants. It can be a nervous experience for a guy,' she said. 'You worry too much. Besides I need the money – remember?'

Something was definitely not right. But if she was comfortable, who was I to argue? 'Well I'll take you in,' I said.

'No need,' she said. 'I'll be fine. It'll help put him at ease. He's in the hands of a professional now.'

She walked methodically to Unit 3, showing the world the accent of her femininity. The punter looked at the ground. He appeared to mumble something at the floor. She walked in first, offering a brief glance back at me. He stared as well as he shut the door behind him. The barely audible click it made fell ominously upon my ears.

Punching the numbers on my phone, I called Sam. 'I'm at Greenlane,' I said, 'but I'm not sure about this one. He's up to something.'

'What do you mean?' Sam said. He did not sound too worried.

'I don't know. Maybe it's nothing, but I'm not sure.'

'Well stick around. We haven't got much for the next hour or so. Sometimes the presence of the car will put them off anything dicey. She's a smart girl as well. She wouldn't have gone in if there was anything wrong.'

'I suppose so.'

'Drop her off back here when you're done. Then you got a pickup in Kingsland.'

I scrawled down the address on the back of the map book and sat back into my seat. The headrest swallowed the back of my skull and eased slightly the tension I felt between the shoulder blades. Looking over at the motel door, I wondered how she was faring. She could have been in danger, but the cheaply constructed barrier of wood, veneer and paint was hiding it from me. Troubled, I turned on the radio, searched for a station, finally choosing one that spoke of cool jazz and long nights.

Reaching into the back seat, I drew forth my satchel. This was the first time in days that I had time to pore its contents. My fingers found one of her diaries – the others were in my Toyota –

feeling the skin of red faux leather momentarily. Then abandoning its touch, I found what I sought. An envelope: canary yellow, creased and rapidly fading. Turning on the light I sifted through the photographs that sat within. I knew which one I was looking for – thought about it since I was woken this morning.

I nearly missed it. Somehow, it had stuck to one of Jo. It was vaguely disturbing that even the celluloid, hard copy memories were starting to deteriorate as well. Carefully I pulled the two photographs apart. They separated with a slight tearing sensation that caused me to grit my teeth and shudder slightly. I would have to take better care of them. Besides the diaries they were the only possessions that had any meaning for me anymore. They were the sum total of my married life. I felt like a bastard for reading her diaries. Even in marriage, I had always felt that couples were entitled to a smidgen of a private life – little pockets of secrecy. I felt a chill, empty wave come over me.

'Bill still misses Jo,' I murmured to myself. It was barely audible, even to my own ears.

The photograph was not part of any secret world - it was Dominic.

His third birthday party. He stood over a cake – bought but home iced by Jo – burning candles waiting to be blown out, looking grand on the plain unadorned table. Little friends were placed around him like pseudo-cherubs on the peripheries. I wondered if these friends still existed in Dominic's world. Dominic's smile was a beacon, a shining lighthouse in my soul. He didn't feel the emotion that troubled his father's mind. Here he would forever be, Dominic the innocent. Dominic the peaceful. Dominic the happy. I had to do all I could to ensure that my dream was fulfilled. It was a father's duty. With what little fatherhood I had left to offer.

So absorbed was I in the image, that I did not notice the figure that approached outside in the darkness. I was made aware as the sharp knock at the window dispelled my reverie and drew me back to the present. I fumbled for the button and the smooth glide of the electric window fell into action.

'There are no vacancies here,' the newcomer said, 'You'll have to try somewhere else.' He was a slovenly man, a loose cardigan, slippered, a slack belly protruding through his buttons. His hair was a horseshoe around the crown, his skin-covered top gleamed. Large plastic rimmed glasses sat on the end of his nose. All that was missing was a folded up newspaper under the arm and the effect would have been complete. Middle age in all its horribleness: cankerous, sickly, tired and on the decline. I would never be reduced to this state, never see the world from those types of eyes. God help me if I did. That would mean I had failed again.

'I'm not looking for a room,' I said, 'My wife is just visiting her brother in number 3. She shouldn't be too much longer.'

'I know exactly what she's doing. I run a respectable establishment here. I pay my taxes and I don't break the law. We don't have your sort around, thank you very much. You'll have to move on.'

'I'm telling the truth,' I said, 'she hasn't seen him for over a year. Give her a break.'

'Then why are you out here. Why aren't you inside playing happy families?'

'Oh, I can't stand him. We haven't spoken for years. So I sit out here, he sits in there and everyone is kept happy. It's simple really.'

It was amazing that the lies were escaping so easily from between the lips. I had never been much of a liar. Could not keep a straight face, or I bumbled my words into a mindless river of drivel.

But the words flowed, my face sailed on an even keel and no neuralgia tics gave this particular game away. It showed on the manager's face. He was not convinced, but he was unsure.

'She shouldn't be too much longer, mate,' I said. 'I'll make sure we make no noise when we leave.' I plastered the most syrupy grin I could master across my face.

Checkmate. His king was trapped. He took a step back, his face a mask of servility, but he still tried to maintain a modicum of dominance. 'See that you do,' he said, 'Have a nice night.'

The manager wandered back to another unit. There was a sort of aimlessness in his gait. He seemed to know he has been duped but he was far too gone to come back in reprisal. As the beaten middle-aged drone entered the door, I caught a brief glimpse of the poor sod's wife. It was a vision of hell. I heard the beginning of a heated debate as the door closed behind them.

I hoped Morgana would be not too much longer. A sneaking suspicion whispered that there would be a reluctant round two, if a certain spouse had her way. I realised I had not worried about Morgana for a while. When had that occurred, when I studied my son's face or during the verbal duel with management?

It did not take much longer. The door to Unit 3 opened and they stepped out. She turned her cheek. He kissed her on it. It was a chaste sort of gesture, the sort of action one observed between adolescents on virginal first dates. Morgana smiled all the way back to the car. Even in the low light, I detected the whiteness of her teeth against the darkness of her lips.

'See I told you,' she said as she got in, 'a pussycat. Sucker even gave me a fifty dollar tip for a quick extra.' She saw the puzzlement in my face and made a shaking signifier with her fist. 'Hand job.'

I turned on the ignition, the car purred into life. 'We got to get you back,' I said. 'I've got to do a pickup in Kingsland.'

We started the meandering course back to Sandringham. She rested herself back and yawned.

'I've got to get some more sleep,' she said. 'I had some stuff to do today and my body-clock's misfiring.'

I remembered my failed attempt at shadowing this morning.

'I saw Jasmine today,' I said.

'That slag. Stay away from her. I don't know her gig. But the boss has something on her.'

'Sam?'

'No your mate, old moneybags. She's trouble.'

As the BMW accelerated up Khyber Pass, I ruminated on a girl in a black peasant dress and a green top. What caught her interest so, in that shop display?

15.

As I drew nearer to my destination I felt my heart drum harder. On the map I had made no connection, but as my ride drew closer to the end of its journey, I guessed where I may end up. Why didn't events run smoothly the way they were planned in my mind? Why was there a complication at every turn? I pulled in at the top of the street.

The street sign was curled up and twisted, hanging by one remaining bolt from the white peeled post. The boredom of youth had laid waste at the city's expense.

I got out.

The rain had begun a slow descent again; the air had the chill bite of a southerly about it. Misty vapour escaped my lips with each exhalation. I walked almost tentatively to the offending sign and made out the letters written upon it. I hoped I was wrong, but my eyes told me that this is just a lost desire. Being at the right place, wanting it to be somewhere different, was not changing the reality of my predicament.

The walk back to the car was even slower. The soles of my new shoes dragged on the cement, my mind not entirely willing their direction or pace. It still could be alright – could have been someone different in some other house, blissfully unaware of the neighbour that dwelt at the bottom of the cul-de-sac.

Starting the engine again, I pulled out from the kerb and turned downwards over the prow of the hill to the great beyond. The motorway was still apparent from the top, the line of cars still made their voyage in a reasonably orderly fashion, the houses still sat darkly on either side of him, my stomach was still left somewhere at the top of the road. I could not make out the numbers on the letterboxes. Why didn't someone do something about the lighting in this fucking street? Anyone could have lurked in the darkness. I parked on the side before the bowl of the cul-de-sac, not wanting to enter that domain if I didn't have to.

I chose a letterbox on the other side of the road. The number I wanted was odd but this side was even. My options were running out. Knowing subconsciously, and just a little bit consciously, what house I had to go to, I whittled away all the possibilities that it was not so. I crossed over.

The number on that box was odd but short of the number that I required. Counting out in sets of two, I realised which one I had to arrive at, my heart sank

I wouldn't drive down further. Instead, I would walk and the damn girl could bloody well walk back with me. Stomping down, through the broken down gate and knocking on the battered door with the broken pane, the trepidation was gone, replaced by anger that I am back here.

'Just get the girl and leave,' I mumbled to myself. I cracked at the door with cold fingered knuckles. The chill of the air made the action painful; the soreness inspired instant regret.

Morty opened the door. All the pent up frustration and the false courage brought about by the short moments of bravado were dispelled by the appearance of him.

'I've come for the pick-up,' I blurted out.

'Why hello, Bill,' Morty said easily. The quiet arrogance dripped around my ears. 'We're fast becoming friends. I had no idea that you would be the one. Good. The last driver that came here was terribly rude. I felt like teaching him some sort of a lesson. Lucky he didn't turn up tonight, isn't it?'

He threw me a wink. Not in the quick, usual sort of fashion, but in a slow deliberate way, almost seductive in its manner.

'Yeah,' I said, 'the girl...is she ready?'

'Of course she is Bill. One thing I am particularly pedantic about is punctuality. There is never enough time in the day to achieve everything I need to do. You for instance, are ten minutes behind time according to my estimation. Bit hectic out there is it?'

'I'm sorry, Mr Mortimer -'

'Morty, please call me Morty. You only get one name remember?' Again the same type of wink was thrown. This man was repugnant. His very words left a sour taste.

'I'm sorry – Morty. We are sort of busy tonight. If I can just pick up the girl, I'll be on my way.'

'How rude of me Bill. I do detest rudeness, particularly in myself. Let me just get her for you.' He disappeared, leaving the door partly ajar. I wondered if the girl was in the room with *Starry Night*, or in some other dank place. Did Morty's distaste for possessions run to not owning a bed? Surely not. I could hear vague, muffled conversation from within, undeterminable in meaning but I detected a threatening manner behind it. Maybe she had lit a cigarette.

The door opened to its fullest extent. There she was. Jasmine looking – as she always seemed to do in my presence – downwards at the floor. She stepped through, so frail that she seemed vaporous like a spirit and stood behind me.

'There she is, Bill,' said Morty. 'My little waif. Ready to take on the world again.' He looked past me at Jasmine. 'So do you feel stronger, petal?'

All that she seemed to be able to muster is a strangled sounding whimper. She sounded like hope lost.

'Aren't you forgetting something, my love?' said Morty. He turned his cheek side on. I detected the beginning of a tattoo just above his collar. Jasmine sidled past me and kissed his face. Morty grasped her chin in his fingers and stroked the hair back from her eyes with the other hand. He looked deeply into them. She seems transfixed, incapable of movement, like a small animal in headlights.

'We better get going,' I said. There was something horrific occurring here and I wanted no part of it. The connection was broken.

'Certainly, Bill,' said Morty. 'We don't want to make you later than you already are. You must come around sometime when you do have time. I'm sure we will have plenty to talk about.'

I was turning and walking away before the door closed. Jasmine was even quicker, through the gate and up the road. 'Where's the car?' she said.

'Other side.'

She was at the passenger side before I had made my way across. Was in the door as soon as the central locking system allowed her fingers to work the latch.

'We'll get you back then,' I said as I worked myself into the seat. The relief that this particular pick up was made, eased the pinching between my shoulder blades and the throbbing in my frontal lobes.

We motored back up the rise, the rubber of the tyre treads initially slipped on the slick surface in my haste to be away. She did not say a word on the ascent. This did not change as we headed back along the New North Road towards Sandringham. What had I done to earn her contempt?

My frustration hit a crescendo and I pulled in sharply to the kerb. A vehicle that followed close behind lets out a wail on its horn: long and temperamental. 'Fuck off,' I screamed at it, lifting my hand in a one-finger salute at the offender.

I turned on Jasmine. 'Look,' I said. 'I'm sorry about following you. I still don't know why I was doing that. But I've only known you a while and you fucking well infuriate me. You don't have to be my friend but let's at least try to be civil. For Christ's sake I've been nothing but polite and the bloody contempt -'

Jasmine body surrendered with a shudder. It took a while for me to realise that she was consumed by silent sobbing. *Fuck*.

'I'm sorry,' I said, 'I don't know what it is, but I always seem to fuck up around you.' I put a hand on her arm to comfort her. She shrugged it off and turned into the door. 'I give up,' I said.

'Take me home,' she said. Her voice was soft, almost childlike.

'Oh, so you do talk.'

'It's not you,' she said. 'It's him.'

'Who? Morty?'

She shuddered. The tears were evident on her cheeks, even under the streetlight.

'What does he do?'

She mouthed the answer silently. It took a second effort for the sound to emerge. 'He likes me to play dead.' She cried loudly. It was mournful, wretched beyond reason. 'Just take me home,' she said between gasps.

'Ok,' I said, 'Just tell me where and I'll take you. I'll have to tell Sam.' I opened the phone.

'Take me home first...then ring him,' she said. 'He'll let me stay if I'm already there.'

'I don't know. We're on the clock.'

She stroked a bony set of fingers along my thigh. 'We could make it a business proposition...'

I lifted the hand firmly from my leg. This woman was truly a fuck-up. 'Look,' I said, 'I'll help you out. Just don't turn everything into a damned game. Where do you live?'

She told me. It was a familiar address. I had already been there once already tonight. This life was incestuous.

'You live with Steerforth?'

She shook her head. 'Same building, different apartment. He gave me the job.'

'Same as me then?'

She shook her head again, this time vehemently. 'I'm no friend of his. I just owe him.'

'How do you mean?' No reply. 'Appearances can be deceiving,' I said. 'I owe him too. Just in a different sort of way.' There was something about her that built the need to confess everything. Maybe because she was one of life's natural victims. Perhaps because I needed to appease her, comfort her, give her some solace in her life. Sighing, I pulled once more into the traffic, u-turned and drove back towards Grey Lynn.

I threw the radio back onto a jazz station. Miles played some haunting melody line, shifting modes at will, soaring angelic then teleporting it back to the gritty depths of the street. My thoughts wandered on the sound, not focused but drifting like a gull in an updraft. Jazz became an escape, a little avenue to duck into and escape the heavy traffic. The monotony of the journey was reduced. Time had folded in on itself and we arrived at the familiar apartment block.

'Do you want to walk me in?' she asked, 'It's not always safe outside.'

'Sure. I've got to tell Sam now though.'

'Tell him later. Just get me inside.' Her voice had become nervous, it had a hysterical aspect.

Getting out, I walked around to her door and opened it for her. Somehow I thought Jasmine expected this. 'I'm ringing once we're inside,' I said.

The foyer to her apartment block was colder than outside. It was basic checkerboard linoleum, grey walled and lowly lit. 'Steerforth lives in here?' I asked.

'He's upstairs,' she said. 'They're a bit more posh up there.'

We came to the appropriate door. She slid her key into the lock and opened it. 'Make your call in here,' she said, 'I think I've got some coffee somewhere.'

The smell hit me as soon as I entered. I had always associated femininity with tidiness, the clean sense of the home in a specific order. This particular fantasy was sharply broken as I entered something that looked surprisingly like a war zone. Clothes lay strewn across the carpet. A couch folded out into a bed displayed a mess of sheet, duvet and magazine spread out across its surface. The wall were singularly unadorned, the plain wallpaper looked jaundiced.

It was one single room. Kitchen met living room met bedroom. Somewhere in here there was food, cooked but abandoned in the mess. I could smell it. It permeated the air, hanging fetid in the atmosphere.

'Jesus,' I said. 'I thought I was bad. You actually live in this shit.'

She shrugged it off, went to a chest of drawers that sat against a wall, and plucked a plain paper bag from within. She hurried into the kitchenette area and turned on an element on a pathetic range.

'I'll just make that call.' I turned away from the mess – trying not to think about it – and focused on the plain excuse of a door. Flipping the phone open, I punched the number.

'Where are you,' Sam said.

I heard Jasmine humming somewhere behind me tunelessly.

'I had to drop her off. She's really upset, mate,' I said.

There was a moment of dead air before he replied. 'What do you mean upset?'

'Upset. Crying. Not well. She isn't capable of working anymore tonight. No good to anyone.'

'Put her on the phone.'

Turning, I found her sitting at the edge of the fold out, a belt looped around her upper arm, a syringe inserted lower down.

'It's not a good time, Sam.'

The hit up complete she swayed momentarily, then toppled back.

'What's up Bill?'

'She's dropped off to sleep. She's a write off for the night.'

'Just come back,' he said, 'I'll deal with it later.'

Shutting down the phone, I walked over to her, a hit of trepidation came upon me. Her chest rose and fell shallowly. Her top had risen up uncovering her belly. I had seen visions like this before – on television – starving refugees, gaunt without hope. The flesh has been sucked away; I easily saw each rib and hollow. Clothed, she had disguised it well. Her face carefully painted to disguise the extent of her emaciation. She merely looked thin not starved and gaunt.

The withering of her body was hard to swallow. But what had been done to it more immediately was unforgivable. Along the lines of what was left of her belly, in perfect rows, stood a pattern of burns. The shape of the outline was rough, but the shape was undeniable. It was a malevolent moon, strikingly similar to one I had seen before.

Gently, I pulled the top down covering the wounds and rolled her on her side. She murmured something soft and unintelligible. I stroked the hair off her face and left, not looking back.

The drive back was done with a cold calculating fury. They were right – all of them. I was not suited to this job.

16.

Two Harleys roared like iron horses out of *Nymphs* car park as I drove in. One rider thrust a heeled boot into my rear fender as they passed me by. The car reverberated with the echo of the steel capped boot, but I barely noticed it. What did I care? It was not my car and I'd not have to drive it for too much longer anyway. The BMW as sleek and prestigious as it was, had become a symbol of what was wrong in this world – the hurt it signified.

This collection of steel, rubber and expensive plastic would be Cutter's property. They were merely destroying what they owned by proxy. People like them destroyed what they touched by nature. That was the theory and theory was all I had to work on. That had always been the problem.

I parked next to my own battered wreck.

It was the first time I had really seen it since I parked it up – was it only a few days ago? I visualised each little ripple in the lines, the patch of rust lining the door sill, the filled and primer swept repair underneath the back window that was slowly being eaten away by the slow advance of rot, the small stone chip in the upper right side of the windscreen. All these things before detracted from its worth.

Now I saw it differently.

Now I saw all the facets that added to the ruin of this sedan as a badge, an insignia that spoke of honesty. Each flaw told a story, an episode that until this point I had not realised. They didn't sum up the whole of my life but they did sum up the last eight years.

Dominic was eight.

This vehicle had seen the entire existence of my son. I had bought the station wagon because that was the sort of vehicle young families owned. It had driven Jo, belly swollen, waters broken to the maternity ward. The passenger seat had probably felt the warmth of the amniotic fluid; bore the brunt of the contraction screams, felt the weight of a newborn son.

The car I sat in now was a sordid present. A vile and bitter gift, slowly filling with cold hatred, of not only them but also slowly myself. I pounded a middle-aged fist against the leather-clad steering wheel.

Slamming the door as I got out, I fancied that the driver's window shook in its tracks against the violence of the blow. I hoped so.

Choosing not to enter the ground floor, I instead traipsed up the stairway to my apartment. I didn't want to face anyone at the moment, preferring instead to hide away from the world even if it was only for half an hour or so. I wasn't tired but I lay on the bed anyway and stared at the dimpled surface of the ceiling. It looked remarkably like a lunar landscape. Not the bitter vision of Mr Benjamin Mortimer – fuck calling him Morty but the practical moon. The moon that operated under one sixth of the earth's gravity, in the vacuum of space, influencing nothing except the tides and the amount of light in the night sky.

The phone rang and I didn't snap it open. Rather, I waited for moments then deliberately pulled the receiver to attention. 'Yeah,' I said in an equally measured fashion.

'Where are you?' Sam said.

'Upstairs. I'll be down shortly. I just needed a few minutes.' Breaking my connection without waiting for an answer, I shook a cigarette from the packet in my pocket and then remembered Jasmine's anorexic midriff: burned and scarred, attached to her body lying comatose in a shitty room, leading a shitty life and not caring. Placing it back into the packet, I crumpled it in a fist, threw it, and buried my head into my hands.

Groaning at the walls, I willed myself up off the bed.

The velvet lady's eyes followed me as I stomped to the office.

'What's the story with Jasmine?' Sam asked.

'She was out to it when I left,' I replied. 'I'm a bit worried about her. She could be sick or something.'

'Fucking junkie bitch. You didn't see her using, did you? I can't abide girls fucked up on the job. It's not professional.'

'No. She was pretty sick. That job of hers...that a regular gig?'

'Pretty much. Most Thursdays. He's a good payer...always books her for four or five hours. Why? Did you have any trouble?'

'No. She seemed a bit upset afterwards that's all. Doesn't like him too much, I think.'

Sam gave a desultory flick of the hand, a brief look of disgust flitted across the broad expanse of his face. 'Everyone upsets her. You've seen her. If it wasn't for Steerforth, I would have kicked her arse out months ago. But he wants her here. He's the boss.'

He wiped sweat from his bald pate, his head gleamed momentarily under the fluorescent light glow. 'So you met Tama. Don't want to associate with those boys. They're family and everything but they're bad news. He seems to have taken a bit of a shine to you.'

'I only met him for a few minutes.'

'That's all it takes from him. He weighs people up pretty quickly, that boy. Probably smells money to be made in you. That's how he sees people.'

'So do you from what I've seen,' I said, probably a touch too quickly.

Sam sat back in his chair, scrutinized my face. His eyes probed me; I looked away into Hayworth's face. She seemed to hold a knowing glance that I hadn't noticed before in her. There was a soft coating of grime across the surface of the still. It needed dusting.

'I'm not Tama,' Sam said. 'I've got a heart.'

'I didn't say you were. It's just that you've got a love of money.'

'You grow up poor, bro. See how your attitude is then.'

'I did.'

The conversation seemed to die in the moment, carried away in communal disagreement. Feeling my eyes droop, a yawn threatened to escape from my throat. It did so; I stifled it with a hand. Last night had taken its toll.

'You look stuffed,' Sam said. I nodded my mind awry in semi-narcosis. 'There are no jobs on at the moment. Just go downstairs and help Monique on the bar. There may be nothing to do down there. But at least you'll look like you're working.'

My mouth yawned again, my hand does not make it to cover my mouth in time. Half an hour before I had been filled with pent up anger, now I could barely summon up any emotion.

I sailed to the bar as if floating angelic on a cloud made of fluffed cotton and valium.

Monique smiled at me as I approached. 'You look done in, love,' she said. 'A bit better than last night though.'

I forced a smile back. The action worked; my tiredness must have added an element of ease to this forced gesture. 'It's been a long couple of days,' I replied. 'Sam says he wants me to help out on the bar. Never done it before...you'll have to show me.'

'Well, as you can see, not much' she said. Monique gestured to the main lounge. It housed three bored, tired looking girls. Two sat in bored conversation, flicking through a magazine. The other looked up to me in hope then down again uninterested as she saw that I was merely another part of the fixtures and fittings.

The room looked larger for its lack of clientele and in a way somewhat drabber. There was no seduction, no magic in a room where there was no one to seduce.

'What do I do then?'

'There's a seat over there. You're manning the bar that's all you have to do.'

A bar looked different from the other side. From the front it was a wall. Formidable to the uninitiated or a prop for those that who needed to ease their burdens, but from the other side it was a utility: it didn't shine with the promise of fruits to be had. It was serviceable, singularly unattractive and had none of the sparkle that the other side advertised. It was amazing that a few short steps could change the perception. I had propped up a few bars in my time but I have never seen one from this angle.

It was a moot point anyway. All that mattered was the solace to be found in the plain, unadorned polyester covered chair that sat in the corner, against a wall under a rather shabby looking framed bar license. I flopped into it, my head swayed slightly as I came to a final rest. Hearing Monique sidle away to join the others in the other room, her voice stood out from the garbled sound of the others. It sat down a notch, maybe because of its maturity, or perhaps because of the strains of ten thousand cigarettes that had slowly reduced her voice box to a shadow of its former glory.

'Another half hour girls,' she said, 'and then you can take the washing down to the laundry. I think if it stays like this we'll be shutting up shop early.'

The conversation blurred into a meaningless melange. I felt my lids becoming heavy; my head began to drop to my chest. I shook myself awake but the journey downwards began to take hold.

The sleep that took hold was shallow, near the edge of consciousness but deep enough for fragments of images to come to mind. They were a slow wink, an empty syringe with a hint of blood in the bottom of the receptacle, a screaming man, a pair of writhing serpents on a pair of milky-white thighs, a face painted with a deeply etched moko. They came at random and sat there for varying lengths of time. There were meanings there, but they floated just beyond the reach of my perception, swirling in and out of focus. If I could have just grasped the meaning, I would be set free. It would be over.

I didn't know how long I was under when I was shaken gently awake. I knew the face smiling gently at me but I just couldn't recall it. 'How long was I out?' I asked.

'Hour or so,' Morgana said. 'We're closing up – nobody's going to come in now.'

'What's the time?' I said, running my hands through my hair and rubbing my eyes vigorously. Stiffly, I stood. 'Fuck this,' I grumbled.

'Around four thirty,' she said, 'What do you want to do?'

'What do you mean?'

'I mean, as of now I'm unemployed. We could fix that situation. I know you like me. Why don't we go to your room? We could do a deal as we are friends and all...'

My look was one of cool appraisal. She was truly beautiful. Would have looked at home in the pages of magazines, advertising products with the fullness of her lips and the pseudo-desire in her eyes. Yes, she was beautiful, but at that moment she was the most unattractive person I had ever laid eyes on since I had returned to Auckland. Is that all she thought I needed out of a woman? Even for a short while. If I wanted to beat off, I would use my hand. Why would I go to the expense of purchasing someone to aid me in something I could do perfectly well by myself?

By no means a prude, I knew there were a lot of men to whom this proposition would be more than an acceptable idea. But did she actually class me among them. Especially as I had seen her work from close quarters all night, knew her attitude to the clients that she serviced. Most of my self-esteem was left back in Levin. But I would hold onto what little I had left.

'No,' I said. 'I'm tired. I just need to get my head down.'

'You sure?'

'Really sure,' I said, trying to keep the distaste from my voice. After all she was beautiful and somewhat friendly. 'Sleep is what I need.'

The lines of her face changed from eagerness to indifference, a gleam died in her eyes. She nodded and left the bar's nether regions.

'Greedy bitch. I told her you wouldn't be interested,' Monique said. She must have been there through it all, beyond the peripheries of my sight. 'She wants the money too much.'

I shrugged noncommittally. 'I've finished for the night then?'

'You sure have, honey.'

The walk back to the room was unhurried. Passing the velvet lady; she smiled at me alluringly. There was something menacing about her eyes.

'Aren't you forgetting something?' Sam called from his office doorway.

'What?'

'You're always forgetting the money, bro.'

17.

'Where is he?'

'Who?'

'You know who. Dominic.'

'What do you care?'

'He's my son. Of course I care.'

She sniffed and pushed the hair back from her face. 'I expect he's off playing somewhere. He comes and goes as he pleases these days...I guess he's his father's son.'

'He's an eight year old boy and you don't know where he is? What sort of mother are you?'

'How many of those eight years have you been around? You've never given him much time beyond weekends. What sort of father are you? You love your fucking cars more than you do him.'

I bit back angry tears – fucked if I would give her anything. 'I had the workshop to give you things. I didn't notice you complaining about the roof over your head – the clothes on your back. I would have given my eyes to spend more time with him but you always wanted more. You were the one with the education – why didn't you get off your arse and get a job?'

'Maybe that's what you should give me then.'

'What?'

'Your eyes.'

I bury my head in my hands. This fucking woman.

Fuck the fat bastard for making her this way.

18.

'Why do you let that woman boss you around?'

'Because she's my wife.'

She nestled in close. I felt the touch of her hair. It flowed like water on my shoulders and with it came the wash of the ocean. 'In my world you could have many wives. You are a strong man.'

'Not strong enough. What would you know? You're a painting – not even real.'

'Does this feel real?' she asked. Her body slid up my back. Nipples hardened against me, my cock mimicked them.

'Yes,' I murmured.

Her body halted its progress. 'Then I'm real enough. Live what you feel.'

'I'm married.'

'Did you ever stop to think that your world is not real and you're my fantasy? Maybe you're stuck in the painting and I'm what exists.'

'No. Paintings don't hurt like I do.'

'Then what is the answer then?'

'Maybe neither of us is real and we're all Jo's dream.'

'Maybe she's not real either.'

'No that can't be.'

'Why not?'

'Because I'd be there to wake her up.'

19.

The beat up sedan had creaks and groans that I had never noticed before. I supposed, they had always been there, but after the luxurious ride of the last few days, the cry of my own motley vehicle was more obvious. When I pressed down on the accelerator pedal, the car did not surge forward eagerly; rather it whimpered somewhat pathetically and dragged itself in the general proposed direction.

There was an old car odour present too, one part damp, one part rotting carpet and two parts carbon monoxide from a ragged hole somewhere along the lines of the exhaust system. In its own way, the sound of the exhaust was a comfort. The sound it made gave my ride an air of false grunt. Young hoons spent thousands of dollars on mufflers to get their cars to sound gruntier. I had spent nothing. This grand secret could have been marketed. Just buy a shitty car and let the elements slowly devour it over long slow years and all their dreams would come true.

Beside me, on the fake lamb's wool seat-cover, lay the map book opened on the correct page. On top of it sat the plain gold-lettered card given to me – was it only two days before? *Benjamin Mortimer, Trader*, along with the harmless Epsom street address. The prospect of having to see him sent me into palpitations.

I was under way.

Driving the Auckland streets by day was an absolute bitch. Manageable by night, the cars flowed evenly. Lines of traffic worked in unison weaving themselves in and out with a minimum of fuss. By day however, the progress was more static, a burst of high energy followed by a swift end brought about by strategically placed traffic lights or the poor foresight of road planners all those years ago when congestion was never an issue.

I let out an almighty, 'Fuck.' as the car stopped on Manakau Road for the fifth time in as many minutes. My fault for choosing to contend with the morning rush hour onslaught. Still, it gave me time to study the map. It's just a matter of timing my reading skills with the lull in movement on the road. Twice now, I had been caught head down in concentration only to be awoken from my task, by the sharp retort of a car horn pressed by a frustrated commuter. Thank God, I chose not to lead the nine to five life anymore – more like an organised slow death than any sort of quality existence.

The turn onto Greenlane West was no better. Traffic was actually heavier making a slower progress to the industrialised areas south. The further south you went, the greater the industry and the greater the amount of poor housing. Not many cafés serving flat whites and lattes to mincing showy patrons down there. Not many discussions on the advantages of apartment living or last July's overseas jaunt when the weather was too cold to bear at that time.

I am certain that there was probably a quicker way to make it to Epsom. To those with the benefit of years of commuter travel there would be a more economical obvious course of action to take. If they knew, they would probably look at me with carefully rolled eyes at the idiotic route I had chosen. But better to go the way I knew and bugger the consequences. I'm on my own time, tired from too little sleep.

Three more dawdling turns and I was on the right road. I almost missed what I was looking for. This area had almost certainly been allocated as a residential domain. The shop I was looking for stood alone and at first glance appeared just like another house. A long glass frontage crammed with everything from old bicycles, table and chair sets, bookcases and smaller bric-a-brac hid the interior from the outside.

Places to park up were in short supply on the roadside. I found a spot a few hundred metres down, just enough room to squeeze between a rusting Holden and a much newer Nissan. My car, set between the two, seemed to bridge some sort of generational gap for automobiles.

The sun advertised artificial warmth to the unsuspecting pedestrian. A cold morning southerly wind infiltrated my suit penetrating the flesh beyond. Shoving my hands into my pockets I leaned into it, each step on the red chip surface a trial against the elements. By the time I reached there, the end of my nose knew the bite of Auckland air.

It was an old fashioned unpainted kauri door that confronted me at the entrance. One only had to look at it to appreciate its weight; the age of it reflected the shop's wares. A turn of the ornate brass handle and I was inside. The dim interior was a swash of old age chaos. Chairs, Victorian prams, even an old roller mower dangled, tied to the ceiling, hung askew at a tangent. The walls likewise displayed shelves at odd heights; atop them were bygone items: books sat next to polished copper fire extinguishers, next to painted metal toys, next to plates and pottery of assorted sizes. In one clear space, in the milieu, stood a tall gaudily coloured toucan statuette, a bright yellow-orange beak shone like a beacon on the unsuspecting customer.

The floor space, as far as I could see, did not have any sort of logical order to it either. There were no rows to demarcate where the patronage should walk and inspect the goods on offer. The pathways offered by the floors were irregular and vaguely elliptical. Tables of various woods and styles: colonial, deco, right through the spectrum to plain old kitsch, served as a base for smaller goods: large nouveau vases, umbrella stands, smaller bookcases and items that I could see no purpose for.

Somewhere beyond all this lay the back of the shop and presumably a counter where the curios on offer could be purchased. Carefully, so as not to disturb anything in the narrow walkways, I cut a path in search of it. I rounded the corner of a particularly haphazard mountain of furniture and ornamentation and found what I had been looking for. Behind a large display case of silverware, promoting jewellery, cigarette cases, tankards and the like, sat a broad mahogany leather-topped office desk. Sitting behind it, hunched like an albino crow was Morty.

Without looking up he said, 'Well, well Bill. Twice in less than twelve hours. I see you used the card.'

'How did you know it was me?'

'You have a very particular sounding walk. Unlike most people you land with the balls of your feet first. It gives you a very peculiar gait and a very distinctive sounding footfall.'

'I used to be hassled at school for running like a girl.'

'They were ignorant. There is nothing very feminine about it. It just displays your character. You are a cautious man and that is displayed by the way you move physically. You just feel out each step with your feet.

'I've never consciously thought about it.'

'That's because you don't live in the now, Bill. I think you live primarily in the past, my friend. That's not a healthy place to be. At the moment you seem to be looking towards the future. If you don't concentrate on the now the future you want may never occur.'

'You seem to know a lot about me,' I said, pandering to this man's giant ego. 'Why do you think I am here now?'

'I think you want me to do something for you, Bill. And I don't think it has to do with that useless proliferation of chattel from this establishment.' This man had the largest case of verbal diarrhoea that I had ever heard. At least Steerforth contained himself to banal simple sentences when he blathered on. This guy was like listening to a dictionary verbalising on speed.

My own speech sometimes bordered on the pretentious, but at least I spouted on a human level most of the time. I didn't need to show my intelligence by displaying it in conversation.

'You're right. I do want to talk to you about a proposition.' Morty eased back into his chair, allowing himself a small smile of satisfaction. It looked like a barefaced grin of death. 'But it's not what you're thinking...' I allow myself a smile. 'How do I know you have cash at your place...a lot of cash?'

His smile stayed but the satisfaction left. The colour drained from his cheeks and the death directed itself at me. 'What do you mean?' he said.

'I said: how do I know about your money? I know it's there and I am only telling you out of professional concern. I don't want to know it but I do.'

'Who -'

'I think you know. But the question is what do you want to do about it? Maybe we both have a mutual interest here. I'd even pay you – I've got money.'

'Ah Bill, you would not believe the depths I travel to. I scare myself sometimes, to coin a phrase.'

'Good. The thing is I don't know this world. What are we going to do? How much will it cost me? What -'

Morty held up his hand. His whisper came as a hiss. 'What's your gig? Why are you so concerned?'

I plastered the grin and put out my hands in offering. 'I'm a henpecked man. The wife won't let me back unless -'

'You're separated -'

'I'll always be married.'

'What do you want done to him?'

'I don't care. I just want him to know. To hear him plead.'

'Why, Bill?'

Shaking my head firmly, I said, 'That's between me and him. Besides, I don't want you after me because of his fucking greed. That's enough in itself.'

'It doesn't really matter why. I've got my own reasons now. We can do it at my place. I'll lay out some plastic tarpaulin to stop any mess we might make. I do so hate an untidy house. We could do it tonight if you like. Around eight o'clock?' He sounded as if he was making arrangements for a dinner party.

'That's all very well, but how are we going to get him there? It's not as if you and I are best friends or anything. He'll know something's up.'

'Us...not friends? I'm mortally wounded, Bill.' Morty placed a hand over his heart and played out a mock swoon. 'But you're forgetting dear old Brian. He's still not paid. Alan will need my services tonight.'

'How much?'

'You can be so banal, talking finance at a time like this. But I suppose we will have to take into consideration that you're an eager young pup.' He sat back in his chair, his eyes took on a faraway tone. After a while they drifted back into the now. 'Seeing as you are going to help out as such. I think we can cut you some sort of discount. So I think an even thousand should do it.'

'Is that all?'

'The market for human suffering isn't that great. Even in a civilised place like this,' Morty said. 'You could probably find plenty who would do it for less – even do it for free. But you would have to slum it and the services on offer aren't too discreet.'

'I can go to the bank now if you want.'

Morty waved his hand negating the intention. 'No need. Pay me on completion of the job,' he said. 'There's one other little thing. I'll need to see my little friend afterwards. I get appetites after a hard nights work. You know what I mean?'

'I'm just the driver. I can ask her, or you can book her and I'll cover the cost.'

'That would be perfect, Bill.' He reached forward and shook my hand. The hand he offered was cold and dry 'Tonight around eight then.'

I couldn't help myself. 'It's a date.'

The cold breeze outside relieved me of the taint of Morty; it washed clean a sense of grime that had seeped its way into the very pores of my skin. I still could not see the inside from here, but I sensed a set of hunter's eyes upon me. It was not until I reached the kerbside, next to the car, that I looked back at the shop front and let out a slow deliberate spit.

Heavy green phlegm sat in contrast to the red chip of the pavement.

***

My watch face told me it was still early – not yet 11a.m. The driver's seat stuck springs into the middle of my back, but it was the most comfortable ride I had in six months.

The car steered itself back towards Grey Lynn. The traffic had lightened, most commuters now sitting crouched over desks or slaving in industry.

I saw Jo in the passenger seat. She smiled at me, hummed to herself a perfect melody. Haunting modal changes. In the rear view mirror, I saw Dominic gazing out the window, playing games with outside suburban landscape: counting the lampposts or naming the streets in his head.

'I love you,' I said.

Jo looks at me her eyes lit sadly. She pointed to her mouth and indicated that she could not reply. Or would not.

Jo looked back out the front of the windscreen. My eyes followed hers. I almost missed the immobile car in front, my foot slammed the brake pedal to the floor. The car tyres screamed, the body drifted slightly sideward.

Screwing my eyes shut, I braced myself for the imminent impact.

It did not come. Slowly opening my lids, I observed that I had missed a collision by mere millimetres.

Jo was gone. Checking the rear view, I saw that Dominic no longer amused himself in the back. Alone once more, I raised my eye skywards and repeated the promise I had made before.

'Soon, baby,' I murmured. 'Soon.'

20.

I wrinkled my nose against the odours I would have to explore when the door opened. That is if it would open. I cracked my knuckles once more on the cheap veneer surface.

Nothing.

Reaching for a smoke inside my jacket, I turned to leave.

'Who is it?' her small voice came from beyond the door.

'It's me.'

The hinges turned and the door opened a crack. 'What do you want?'

'Let me in. I've got a proposal for you.'

The crack widened. I could see her elfin face: bleary eyed, hair tousled and eyes shot red. 'What proposal?' she said.

'Let me in and I'll tell you.'

The crack widened to a chasm and the smell of weed intensified. Painting a smile across my face, I stepped past her into the chaotic interior.

Magazines that only covered segments of her bed the previous night, now plastered the entirety of the surface. On top of them lay a pair of scissors. From the highly glossed pages, pictures of models had been cut and arranged in a rough stack at the edge of the bed. A couple of loose pages lay on the floor on top of a pair of black-laced panties. The holes rent in the paper made the pages seem naked.

She was wearing a t-shirt, pastel pink with a tiny golden teddy bear embossed over the left breast. It ended high on her thighs. Her legs still hadn't been sucked of the flesh the rest of her body had been deprived of. They still looked full. If I didn't know what lay behind the thin cotton, I would have found her desirable.

Jasmine let out a sigh and bowed down over the bed and in a single motion, swept the bed of magazines.

'How long do you want?' she said.

Her bony hands begin to pull the shirt over her head. Pink cotton rode over her hips. She was wearing nothing beneath. Her pubis was freshly shaved clean. The sight gave the illusion that her body belonged to someone much younger.

'No,' I said. The reproach came a lot louder than I intended. Grabbing her forearm, I stopped the inevitable progress. I did not want to see the burn scars– not in the light of the new day.

Jasmine flinched from my clutch. A look of brief horror spread across her features.

'No,' I repeated, this time gently. I released her arm. She sat on the bed. 'Not with me.' I said.

'Not good enough for you,' she said. Her eyes swept up suddenly in a burst of anger.

'It's not that. You remind me too much of someone, that's all. Way too much.'

The irritation drained from her face as well as some colour. 'So do you,' she said.

Replacing my hand on her arm, I wiped strands of loose hair from her face. It shamed me to manipulate her this way. Singly, she was the most interesting person I had met in years. Another time or place, I would have befriended her. Maybe more.

'How would you like to be rid of him?' I tried to put every inch of a softness in my throat. Jasmine's head rose slowly. 'You'll have to go back one more time though. Can you do that, you think? I asked.

She nodded. Just barely. A small droplet of a tear appeared in the corner of her eye. A rare jewel glistening on a dusty floor. She trembled. I extended my arm around her sparse shoulders.

Jasmine broke away. 'I need to fix,' she said.

'You don't have to, you know.' A glow of tenderness dropped over me. I had only felt this with one other.

A sneer transformed her high cheek-boned face into something ugly. 'You asked me why I don't like you. It's because you can't fucking accept what I am. I see it in your face, those bloody puppy dog eyes. This is what I am.' Her hands spread wide over her head. 'A junkie whore. Nothing else. I'm not who you want me to be. I'm not what anyone wants me to be. Not unless you've got the money -'

I stopped her short. Placed my hands on her cheeks, closed my eyes and kissed her on those cherubic lips. Her body fell limp for seconds then tightened as she returned in kind and took over. A hesitant tongue pushed its way past my teeth to explore my own. Lips parted, my eyes locked onto hers, my hand reached out and caressed her cheek

She fell back on the used sheets as I guided her down gently. Raising her t-shirt, so it rested above her pelvic area but below the blight left on her by Morty, my lips brushed the inside of her thigh then wandered to the centre, the tongue sought out and worked on her clitoris, making little circles. Saliva blended with the essence of her, eliciting a salty-sour taste. Her bare mound prickled against my nose.

Barely audible moans escaped from Jasmines far off mouth. I sensed her ragged breath heightening. Every part of me poured into my action.

Stopping, I raised my head, unbuckled and worked my trousers down. The action was cumbersome; no Casanova was I. Never had been. Looking into her eyes again, I pressed my lips back on hers and gently worked myself inside her.

It was not fucking – not love making, but something in between, slow, each push and withdrawal pursued carefully. Closing my eyes, I relived the experience once more and abandoned myself to the past. In a Levin bedroom with lemon wallpaper, a bed with warm cotton sheets and floor devoid of dirty clothes. Tears rolled off my cheeks and splashed downwards.

I came – the elation long but not so joyous. My eyes opened and looked down.

Tears had dropped onto her face, the sadness contained within them seemed to reflect themselves in her own blue-grey orbs.

Kissing her a last time, I snuggled down behind her. My cock pressed her buttocks.

I said, 'We'll do it tomorrow. One more time and he'll never bother you again. Does he really have money stashed away in there?'

'In his wardrobe in two schoolbags,' she said. 'He goes there when he pays me. Says he has a stash because he doesn't own anything.'

'How much?'

The elevation of her shoulders tells me she didn't know. 'I need to fix,' she said and rolled of the bed to the kitchenette.

Watching her from my perch on the bed, cooking on a scorched spoon, drawing the contents through the filter, into a syringe, Jasmine faced away from me as she shot up. She dropped away when she finished, managed to nestle against me in her former position. Comatose in seconds, I felt the slow exhalation of her breath work from her lungs. It drew sleep to the lids of my own eyes. Closing them momentarily, I snapped them open again.

It wasn't Jasmine any longer.

Jo rolled over, her head atop the pink T shirt. Her eyes sifted my thoughts. They delved deep; an astringent feeling of shame filled me.

'You had to do it. Did you think of me when your eyes were closed?'

Tears rolled now freely. When was the last time I had cried?

'I tried to. I'm finding it hard to remember what you look like.'

Her visage blurred then sharpened once more into focus.

'Did you ever look this way?'

'I look the way you want me to look. If you want I can look like her.'

'No,' I replied too quickly. 'Never that. She's her own person. Not you.' I felt my forehead wrinkle, sniffed up my nose what the tears have left, sucked up my breath and tell her, 'I don't know if I am strong enough. I can't go through with it.'

'So love fades with the memory of me. If you don't do it, you'll never see me again. You won't see Dominic.' Her voice was a sharp retort like a stone resounding off an impending windscreen.

'Where is he?'

Jo's face did not change; rather it shifted in a blur, the slight play of a smile on her mouth. 'Playing. He always plays now. No father figure to keep him in line.'

Irritation, a sudden hit, bounced up from my guts. 'You would never have used him as a weapon,' I said 'I wonder if it's even you anymore.'

'Stay with the whore then. You suit each other. Maybe you should just open your eyes.'

My eyes did just that.

Jasmine's gently breathing form greeted me.

'You have turned me into her,' I whispered softly.

Reaching across, I placed my lips in a soft kiss on the rise of her shoulder and extricated myself slowly. Drawing up my trousers – which still rested around the back of my calves – I rolled quietly off my side of the bed and stood without disturbing the dip too much. By mistake, I kicked the chrome scissors hard against the far wall. A metallic and wood clatter woke her.

Jasmine rolled over. Her eyes questioned, then look hurt 'You're going to go?' she asked.

'Yes.'

'Are you going to come back?'

'Tomorrow. We'll get it done. Then we'll see where we can go from there.' I felt a slow build-up of bile from the half-truth.

'I've never had it quite like that before,' she said.

The hope in her eyes churned my stomach violently. All I could manage is a quick, 'See you tomorrow' before rushing out of the dingy interior, down the long corridor and once more into the glare of the continuing day.

Vomit poured from my insides into the gutter alongside the kerb. Shame nipped at my intestines, tearing at them, flooding my insides with the hard bite of acid throwback. Hands pressed down on my knees as my body heaved and retched itself dry, then continued to convulse. Tears would not bother me again, but their stain had left a mark upon me. When had I become so righteous?

The melodic trill and the vibrate touch of the phone went off in my trouser pocket. The same trousers that had sat around my ankles while my cock persuaded a victim with the precision of Mengele. Plucking it free, I answered with a terse, 'What is it?'

'What the fuck are you doing down there?' Steerforth's boom crackled across the airwaves.

'Came to see you.' My voice box was sandpaper dry and damaged. 'But then I remembered I don't know what apartment you live in.'

'Come up. Sixth floor – 613.' The tone of worry was apparent across the receiver. 'Something's come up,' he said, 'You'll have to use the stairs. Elevator is on the fritz.'

The stairs were wide and had not come into consideration when they made this building. They were bare concrete with a rough stone finish, placed on a steel frame. Builders had even ignored the courtesy of smoothing the finish off. The steps echoed on the way up giving me the sense that I was entirely alone here. Halfway up, the bottom door slammed shut; a second set of footsteps resounded in counterpoint to my own. They stopped before I made it to the top, short of breath and feeling tired.

I knocked at 613, on a door that seemed grander than Jasmines just six floors below. Paint graced its surface for a start and a buzzer existed with an ornate gilded cover-plate. I did not get a chance to try it out for sound, being ushered in by a red faced Steerforth.

The interior was black leather couches, white walls and minimal art. Sparse surroundings for the garish man. There were even books lined on the wall. I scanned a few. Copies of Nietzsche, Plato and Rousseau lived alongside Dickens, Hemingway and Flaubert, not arranged in any specific theme as if they had been chosen merely on the merit of the names that housed the bindings. I did not imagine Steerforth had even looked upon the covers; let alone opened them to peruse the contents behind them. The thin coat of dust that covered them confirmed the notion.

'Sit down, sit down,' Steerforth said. 'Wanna drink? I've only got Scotch...'

Shaking my head, I sat myself down on the low-slung cowhide settee. It was not built for comfort. Even with my short stature, I found my knees pulled up towards my chest in this position.

'What's up,' I said, 'you look a bit worried.' Somehow I felt the tables were turned. In the world of primate authority I had become the alpha being – even if it was only in my own mind. Then again maybe it was only smugness.

'It's Brian,' Steerforth said, 'I can't track him down. I've got to get the money or it's on my head. They'll take everything – the parlour. I'll have nothing left.'

'Relax it's what you came into the world with anyway.' It was a powerful feeling, having some sort of upper hand. I had not had the pleasure for a long time.

'You said you have money saved away. Couldn't you sub us it? Just until I get a bit more financial.'

'I couldn't get hold of it for at least a week,' I lied, 'maybe even more. It's all tied up you see – investments. I could perhaps get it for you then.'

'That's no bloody good,' Steerforth shouted. He dug around in his pockets, brushing up and down the fabric of his trousers. 'Have you got a smoke?'

'Sorry mate, smoked my last on the way over.'

I thought of the near full packet in the pocket of my jacket and tried to ignore the thrill of nicotine withdrawal that came with the image. 'I could go down the road if you want. Get some.'

'Fuck, I've got more important things to contend with than bloody cigarettes. They'll take everything off me if I don't track down Brian.'

'Who?'

'Who do you think? Tama and his fucking arsehole Cutters. Why did I let Sam talk me into going into business with them?'

'From what I hear, you were the one who wanted that.'

'Whose side are you on? That queer bastard?'

'I'm on my side, mate. Always have been. Like I said I'll help you if I can. Couple of weeks or so...What's wrong?' Steerforth's cheeks turned a deeper shade of red. He rubbed at his chest.

'Nothing, nothing,' he replied. 'Just a bit of indigestion. What am I going to do?' His voice had the air of a small child with nowhere to turn.

'What about Morty?'

'Morty – yeah Morty. He could help out. Has the knack that boy.' Hope sprang back into Steerforth's voice. 'I'll ring him now.'

'I'll be off then.' I said, not trusting myself to stick around for the call. Steerforth didn't notice me as I walked to the door.

'Hey, Myers,' Steerforth said as I turn the handle.

'What?'

'What did you come over for? You never told me.'

An unseen hand squeezed my guts tight. 'Nothing much. Just seeing what you were up to. Nothing else.'

'Oh – Thanks anyway. I haven't said it yet. But thanks for sticking around. You were the only bloke I ever thought of as a friend.'

As the door closed behind me, I mumbled to myself, 'Am I just.' Was this the right thing I was doing? Not so sure, as I hit the top landing of the stairs.

'Do it for me...'

Peering down the stairwell, I caught a glimpse of Jo looking up. There was disdain in her expression. She flitted away in an instance. New determination instigated my echoing steps downwards.

21.

'Tell me again,' I said.

'How many more times?'

'I need to hear it again. I don't like him but I need to hate him. Tell me what he did to you.'

Her eyes glistened and she gave that smile that never failed to belittle me. 'Anyone would think you got off on this, Bill. What goes on in that filthy -'

I pulled her up short. 'Not even in jest, Jo. I'm never that bastard. Just remember who got him out of your life the first time.'

'You got me away from him. But you didn't get him out of my life. You know that. Now you've got him in yours. It gnaws at you doesn't it?'

'Tell me.'

'I said no...but he did anyway. Then he threw me out his door and he laughed at me. As I said...how many more times?'

'Why didn't you tell me then? Why did you wait all these years?'

'What would you have done? You fucking idolised him. You're struggling now.'

'I would have done something.'

'Why? You're just as bad. You just took fifteen years to use me up and spit me out.'

'I fucking tried.' I closed my eyes against the tears. 'I love you.'

'No you don't. You love the idea of me. Those fucking movies you play in your head. Well now I'm a movie too. Just one you can't control.'

'That's not true.'

'I get to decide that now.'

'I would have done something.'

22.

'I've gotta quit,' I said.

'What?' said Sam.

'I'll work the shift out.. it's not me. I've moved my gear out next door - things play with my conscience a little bit too much here.'

Sam smiled. 'I wondered when you would come around. I don't know what Steerforth was thinking when he brought you in. One look and I could tell the job wasn't for you.'

'I can give you the money for the clothes if you want...'

Sam waved his hand. 'Keep it. It's the fat wanker's money anyway,' he said, hitching his trousers over his own ample belly. 'You don't even have to work tonight if you want. I'll do it.

Business has been so slow lately I just sit in my office and gain weight anyway.'

'No, that's okay,' I said. 'I said I'd do tonight.'

'What are you going to do now? Have you thought about my offer? Not as much money but it's a steady flow of cash. We all need that in life.'

'I'll think about it. Don't know yet.'

'I've got to get hold of the damn place yet. That Gregory is a stoic fucker. Getting him to give it up could take months. Maybe I'll have to squeeze a sale out of him.'

'I haven't told Steerforth.'

Sam winked. 'I try not to give him any bad news. Not unless I absolutely have to. He's been calling for you.'

'I drive him more than I do the girls.'

'Not for much longer. Count your lucky stars.'

'That I do, Sam. That I do.'

***

The drive to Grey Lynn was a calm one. It was too late to turn around now and give up the ghost. It seemed months, since I sat on a marble bench on K Road, staring at indifferent trash through dingy windows. It had only been days and a new century began tomorrow.

Rain began to spatter on the spotless windscreen. Someone had gone to the trouble of cleaning it. Probably Sam. The meticulousness of someone who went to the trouble of personally dressing an employee would certainly bother cleaning the company car as well.

Parking up outside the now familiar apartment block I looked up and spotted the window of his apartment. Behind the well-lit glass, I spied his fat silhouette. Pressing my hand down on the steering wheel, I gave a quick two toots on the horn to announce my presence. His shadow did not move from its position. I sucked back a breath and psyched myself for the long climb up the back staircase.

Breathless by the time I reached the sixth floor, I stopped, bent over, caught gulps of air to soothe my aching lungs and loosen the nicotine butter. Cigarettes would be the death of me. I banged on the door.

'Where the hell have you been,' said Steerforth, as he yanked it open. 'Your phone switched off or something? I've been calling for hours.'

'I'm sorry, mate. The battery must have died – here now anyway.'

'Fucking incompetent,' he said, then pressed his hand on his sternum. 'Bloody heartburn...We've got to go. Morty was expecting us twenty minutes ago. He doesn't like it when you're late.'

'Don't want to keep the man waiting then,'

Ah, the sweet irony.

Climbing down the stairs, Steerforth had to stop and catch his breath, his face a muddy grey pallor, paling even the veins in his cheeks. 'Did you get any smokes today,' he asked.

I passed one from my pocket and handed over a lighter.

Steerforth sat on the stairs and puffed deeply. 'We'll have to stop somewhere and get something for this indigestion,' he said.

'We'll stop at the gas station at the top of Morty's road."

'Just let me finish this and I'll be right.'

We sat in the concrete stairwell where even our silence seemed to echo off the bare walls. *Not long to go now you fat fuck.*

I looked skywards, up the stairs, following the track of the banister and she was there, up on the next landing. She smiled at me and mouths in a silent way, *'My love...'*

She glided sinuously down each individual step towards us.

'C'mon lets go,' I said. 'Don't want to keep the man waiting.' Guiding Steerforth down, a firm hand on his back, I looked behind.

She was no longer there.

We passed into the corridor, Steerforth's laboured breath rattling off the walls. Jasmine's door opened a sliver as we passed on by. Steerforth stopped and pushed the door open. Jasmine fell backwards and caught herself a few steps behind. She was still wearing the t-shirt from that morning.

'Why the hell aren't you at bloody work?' Steerforth roared. 'You're no fucking part-timer. You owe me you lazy bitch.'

Jasmine's bottom lip started to quiver noticeably. 'I...I'm feeling sick.'

'Too sick to lie on your back, fake a moan or two? Get your arse in there.'

'I don't want to.'

'I don't want to,' Steerforth said in mock parody. 'I don't fucking want to do a lot of things. But I have to. Get dressed and we'll drop you off.'

Placing my hand on Steerforth's shoulder, I pulled him around. His face was a grey mask. 'What?' he said.

I stabbed my watch with an index finger. 'Morty – remember? We haven't the time for this.'

'Yeah – alright,' he replied. He turned back on Jasmine who stood, visibly shaking. 'I don't wanna hear tomorrow that you didn't turn up. You know what happens.'

Jasmine cringed even further away: a wilting flower in the scorch of a hot sun.

'Let's go,' Steerforth said.

We turned away back into the corridor. Looking behind me back at Jasmine, I mouthed a silent: 'Tomorrow.' A look especially reserved for angels and martyrs was etched into her face. The barest nod is all I got back and even then I wasn't sure.

At the car, Steerforth waited impatiently for the driver to open the door.

'We're thirty minutes behind,' I said.

'If you had your fucking cell on,' Steerforth panted, 'we would have been early, you useless bastard.'

I opened my door, thrusted myself inside, took my time unlocking Steerforth's side and took a more leisurely time to turn the ignition and fire the car into action.

Nothing was said until the car passed Arch Hill.

'Did you know, I never really knew Jo?' I said.

'What are you talking about?'

'I never really knew her.'

'Who the fuck cares,' said Steerforth.

'I do. She told me you knew her though. Drove her nuts.'

'I tell you what – you're driving me nuts at the moment. We're late.'

Dropping my foot down, the BMW roared forward in sharp reply. Pursing my lips together, I forced a silence for the moment. My teeth began to chew the tender insides of my cheeks. 'Drove her crazy too – eventually.'

'Is that right?' said Steerforth. He sounded bored.

'Yeah. At first I thought it was me that was the crazy one. Her moods, nothing ever good enough. I know better now. She was the mad one. Driven to it you might say.'

'I'm sure I don't know, Myers. All I care about is getting the money. Know what I mean? I don't care about your fucked up wife.'

'Really? That surprises me – after all you helped make her that way.'

'What do you mean?'

'I just thought she was damaged goods. I thought after a year or two she was over it. I never knew though.'

'I don't understand.'

We passed Ponsonby Road and entered the beginnings of K Road. The dark end of the street where the lights were not bright and on the corners, women and drag queens stood in search of customers amid the brilliant headlights that traversed its length. The rain had begun to drop again. It must have been cold, bound to the road in the chill wind that buffeted the legs in cheap nylon, sitting below too short skirts. But I cared nothing about that.

'She told me in the ward beside her bed,' I said. 'Couldn't believe it at first but she made sense. I always wondered why she didn't like you.'

I spotted her in the backseat through my rear view mirror. Jo leaned forward, her face filling the frame. 'Tell him – tell him it all.'

'I am,' I replied irritated, 'will you let me get on with it?'

'Who the fuck are you talking to?' Steerforth said. 'What are you on?'

The car turned right onto Symonds Street and picked up more speed as it gunned over the motorway overpass. Lights indicated green for us to go through at the end, however as we accelerated faster up the rise, the Newton Road intersection lights signalled to stop. The BMW did not. Instead, it gained speed as it drew nearer the lights.

'What are you doing?' Steerforth screamed.

We sped through; car horns squawked, tyres screeched valiantly but no sounds of impact answered us. No victims from the carnage; none that I knew about anyway, we were already gunning for the next set of lights at Mt Eden Road. They came as a red beacon. Ripping the handbrake up, the car skidded straight for metres then stopped, its front wheels a smidgeon over where they should be.

'That's what she did,' I said, looking straight ahead. 'Except she stopped on a lamppost and Dominic died in the impact. It wasn't an accident. No skid marks, you see. She took a little longer to go. So I sat with her and she told me.'

Looking over at Steerforth, I see he was sitting forward in his seat, hands clasped up against his chest.

'What's wrong? Nothing smart ass to say?'

'I can't breathe properly. Get me to a hospital.'

'Maybe it's the guilt acting out – for what you did.'

'I'm serious. Get me there.'

'Morty first,' I mimicked. 'He doesn't like to be kept waiting.' I could do a fair vocal impression.

Steerforth let out a moan and flopped his head to his chest.

Shaking him hard, I said, 'Don't cut out on me now, Alan. Why did you do it?'

Steerforth raised his head slowly. 'I don't know what the fuck you are talking about,' he said. 'I only met her a few times and you were there. Don't fucking call me, Alan.' His eyes fixed themselves forward and he was gone. The ragged heavy breaths ceased and there was quiet.

He was dead.

He couldn't be gone. The fucker couldn't escape me now. I punched him in the face. Once. Twice. Then unleashed myself upon him, smashing, tearing and clawing. 'Killed her slowly for years, you fuck. You can't run away. You have to suffer...' I howled at the windscreen.

A car horn squawked and its sound brought me back. Guiding the car forwards, I aimed it down past Eden Terrace towards Kingsland. A winding narrow stretch, each lane too thin to comfortably house a car, harder to negotiate in night, wet asphalt reflecting and distorting the light patterns, clouding the way onwards.

Steerforth's head lolled forward to his chest once more, bouncing and bobbing with the rhythm of the road. Thank Christ he used the seatbelt, limbs would be flying everywhere otherwise. There was no hesitation this time burying the car down Morty's road. Parking outside the address, I felt no fear walking to his door.

Morty opened it. 'Where is he then?' he whispered.

'In the car.'

'What's he doing there?'

'He's dead.'

'You did it yourself?'

I shook my head. 'Heart attack or something – I don't know. He's still strapped in.'

'This I have to see for myself,' Morty said eagerly. He pushed past me and scuttled on legs to the car. 'He certainly doesn't appear too alive,' he said, peering through the passenger window.

Opening the door, he checked for a pulse on the fat neck, then prodded and poked at Steerforth, pushing his head to the other side. It flopped over like a broken marionette. He turned to me. 'You're a bit of a dark horse – aren't you Bill? I've never seen a dead body up close before.'

I'm gobsmacked. 'What do you mean? I thought you're some sort of expert.'

'I've broken people, for him,' he said, nodding at the corpse, 'but do you think this is a movie or something? I'm a trader not a killer.' Morty's voice sharpened. 'I still want the cash though – for the inconvenience.'

'Relax.' Pulling a plastic bag with the ten hundred dollar bills from my jacket pocket, I tossed it over. 'I need to get rid of him – you can give me a hand. Where do you go to get rid of bodies?'

Morty jabbed another finger into Steerforth's side. 'He had a heart attack – didn't he? We could just dump him back at home – natural causes and all that. No one would be the wiser.'

'Have you seen where he lives? Six fucking flights of stairs.'

'Got a better idea? We could leave him in there, I suppose but I think it maybe a touch too public.'

Fuck. Fuck. Fuck. 'We'd better get on with it then. You'll have to get in the back.'

'At least it will be a quiet ride. No Alan to disturb my peace.'

***

We drove back on a trip that I was beginning to perceive as an eternal loop. The car was guided by my subconscious.

Morty whistled an unmusical tune in the backseat. All I knowingly saw was the regular passing of streetlights on concrete poles. There were a lot of streetlights between here and Grey Lynn –I spotted them all.

Stopping before the apartments, I turned the car off, let my head sink to the steering wheel and drew even breaths, trying to keep to the task at hand.

'Alan's not going to get up there by himself, Bill.'

'I'm thinking how we are going to actually get him up there without anyone noticing. Have you even thought about that?'

'Temper, temper, Bill,' Morty said. 'Actually, I think of situations like this all the time. Don't you, killer?'

'I didn't kill him.'

'Sure you didn't. How about we get either side of him an arm over each of our shoulders and walk him up like a drunk. I'm sure he has come in here that way, many times.'

'Up six flights? I'm not that bloody strong.'

'I'm sure desperation will give you strength, Bill. Better up there behind closed doors than down here in the open.'

Our respective doors opened and shut with a dull thud. Opening the passenger door, I unclipped Steerforth's seatbelt. He fell out the side, clipping me low on the legs causing me to fall back partly underneath him. I scrambled out of the tumble quickly, let out a frustrated 'Shit' and moved to grab the body under the shoulders. Looking up at Morty who is looking on with a slight smile, I said, 'Are you going to give me a hand or what?'

'For a quiet person, you're a funny guy, Bill.' He bent down on the other side of the body. Together we hoisted Steerforth up to a standing position, already he felt cold to the touch.

Carrying him towards the doors was problematic. His legs dragged behind him making him seem twice as heavy. Dead weight. Steerforth had become a smelly cumbersome overcoat.

'Lift him higher off his feet,' said Morty, 'it'll make him easier to carry.'

'You lift him higher.'

From the shadows of the apartments, a bent figure emerged. In the dark, Brian appeared pathetic, one arm a hump underneath a cardigan, the other clutched a plastic shopping bag. His steps looked painful. 'Is that you, Steerforth?' he asked.

'He's a bit under the weather at the moment, Brian,' I said. My heart was thumping but still playing out the part. 'Come to give us something, I hope.'

'I'm five spot short,' Brian whimpered. 'I need another day. I can get it tomorrow morning.

'Well Steerforth's out to it at the moment. You'll have to ask him later.'

'Is he okay?' Brian asks, peering closer at them, 'He looks fucked.'

23.

Looking over at Morty, I clocked him struggling under the weight. 'Have you got him?' I said.

Morty nodded back, grunting slightly under the stress, as I unloaded myself.

'It's like this, Brian,' I said.

'You stay away from me,' Brian said, retreating quickly.

'I'm not going to hurt you. I'm trying to help you, you silly prick.'

Brian faltered, looking hesitantly back at me. 'You sure?' he asked.

'See that fat bastard. He's not going to be happy when he finds out. How much you got in there?'

'Fifteen grand.'

'Take out a grand.'

Brian dropped the bag and fumbled inside the used plastic. 'I've only got one arm.' Loose notes fluttered free onto the damp ground. 'I can't see. I need some light,' he wheedled.

'Take a guess. He could come out of it any minute.'

Brian pulls out a fistful and thrust it in a pocket.

'Now,' I said, 'I suggest you get the fuck out of Dodge. You know it won't be me coming to find you – don't you?' Brian nodded. 'Good. Leave the bag there and bugger off. Understand?'

'Yeah...what about my business?'

'I would have thought breathing and walking properly would be more important to you. Besides, Steerforth says these things run themselves. Think of it as a holiday. An anonymous holiday.'

Brian looked decidedly undecided. 'But what -'

'Let me deal with him, Bill,' said Morty.

'No that's alright,' said Brian quickly.

Dropping the bag, he moved awkwardly onto the street. His retreating form blended back into the shadows eventually.

Picking up the bag and unlocking the passenger side, I placed it on the seat.

'Don't want to bother you, Bill,' Morty said a hint of strain in his voice. 'Steerforth is rather a big bloke, you know.'

Taking up the burden one more, I hoisted my shoulder into the underarm and lifted Steerforth stable. He still smelt of Old Spice and cigarettes. Getting him through the doors proved difficult. It was a balancing act propping Steerforth up with one side of my body and pushing open the double wooden doors with the other. The task was too hard, the body flopped face first onto the cool linoleum.

'Fuck,' Morty said. The first time I have heard him curse since we met.

Dragging him, the linoleum aided our progress, greasing the friction barrier. Moving rapidly down the ground floor corridor, I glanced at Jasmine's place – her door was firmly sealed shut. Wondering if she went in tonight, I turned away. Literally crashing through the end doors, we entered the stairwell. The interior was not any more polished since I had left before.

I dropped my side of Steerforth's body.

Slipping from Morty's hands, Steerforth didn't flop to the ground, rather his knees temporarily took his weight and he sat down slowly with an almost considered air.

'I've got to have a break,' I said.

'It's a risk being out here for too long, Bill,' Morty said. 'We don't want to get caught.'

'I don't really care.'

It was a quiet Friday night in Grey Lynn and I was getting used to this.

Feeling the need of a cigarette to wash away the scent of corpse, I drew one out. The packet was crumpled from Steerforth's bulk. Managing to find one of the few left still intact, I sparked it up and drew deep.

'You know my feelings on smoking inside, Bill.'

'You're on my time now,' I replied, once more mimicking Steerforth – I was getting really good at that. 'A cool grand for lifting him up a flight of stairs. I think I'm allowed a little luxury here and there.'

Morty didn't reply, instead evaluated me coolly. The faintest sheen of sweat pebbled his forehead.

Taking a few luxuriant seconds to take a drag, enjoying the blended flavour, I threw the half-finished effort down onto the concrete floor and squashed it in with my new Italian shoes. Stooping down, I pulled Steerforth up once more, ignoring the strain.

'Are you going to give us a hand, or what?' I said.

Still saying nothing, Morty took up the burden of the other side and we hit the first flight. On the third floor that we stopped again, my thighs were burning from battling uphill. I wished that I had taken more of a rest below and had not chosen to light up.

'We'll just drag him up the rest of the way,' Morty said. 'There's no one around.'

'What if someone does turn up?'

'Like you say, I'm being paid to get him up there. How I do it is up to me.'

'On your head then.'

'And yours.'

Picking Steerforth up under the arms, we dragged him headfirst up the stairs once more. Progress was definitely quicker this way. There was a sound of ripping fabric and Steerforth's shirt lifted out of his trousers exposing one white pendulous belly. Prone, he reminded me of a hairy grub.

'You're just as much hassle dead, you prick,' I said.

'So true, Bill,' said Morty. He delivered a quick kick into Steerforth's legs and threw me an insipid wink. 'Just for luck.'

Making it finally to the top floor, we hauled him outside of his door. Further down, an elderly man with a towelling robe wrapping him up and tartan-designed slippers on his feet opened his door.

'What are you fellas up to?' he asked.

'The man can't hold his liquor,' Morty answered. 'Just doing the right thing and getting him home safe.'

It seemed ridiculous. We were so obviously dragging a body around. But back in the day, this must have been the way to transport drunks, because the old codger merely nodded.

'We'll see that he doesn't make any noise this weekend. Tell him we'll ring the cops, this time. My wife needs her sleep. We're too old -'

'Oh, I'm pretty sure you'll be in for a quiet weekend,' Morty said. 'In fact, I can almost guarantee it.'

The bugger sniffed and returned from whence he came, shutting his door firmly behind him. Steerforth had obviously come home looking like this before.

'Close thing,' Morty said. 'We better get him inside.'

'The keys will be inside his pockets.'

'You can get them,' Morty said. 'I'm coming to the conclusion, that I don't like corpses much. They don't scare – no fun in that.'

Pushing Steerforth up against the nearest available wall, I scrambled around in his coat pockets to no avail.

'Must be in his trousers,' Morty said.

'No kidding. Hold him up will you.'

Morty rested his forearm under Steerforth's chin, holding him up against the corridor wall. I felt around in the trouser pockets and pulled out a plain leather wallet, loaded with cash. Finally the clink of keys sounded and I felt the coldness of the key chain. Pulling them out, I opened up and we wrestled the fat bastard inside. He made a dull plop as he fell on the tasteful carpets.

Falling on the low leather couch, I sucked in deep breaths. I'd never been a fit bloke, not particularly sporty at any time in my life. My shoulders burned across my back and a cigarette now would kill me.

'We can't leave him there,' I said.

'Why not?' said Morty.

'It doesn't look right.'

'What do you mean? Why can't he die there right on the floor – or do heart attack victims have to die somewhere specific.'

'I don't know - let's put him on the couch.'

'You're the strangest man I've met in a while, Bill.'

'This is a strange world.'

We rolled Steerforth up onto the couch. I put a pillow under his head and he looked comfortable. Placing the television remote in his fingertips, I stood back and looked upon my creation.

Something was missing. I studied the room until it came to me. Reaching onto the bookshelf, I plucked down a copy of Rousseau, blew the dust off the cover, opened it at a random chapter and plopped it on top of his belly. It seemed appropriate, in that certain way I perceived the world.

'Very artistic, Bill. I don't get the book.'

'No, you don't.'

'What about his wallet?'

Looking at the flat leather pouch lying alone on the floor, I said, 'I'll put it back.'

'You may as well grab the cash. There's a few hundred there. Treat yourself to a little perks.'

'I don't know...'

'Do you think Alan has any use for it anymore? Go on you know you want to.

Fuck it. It would get me full tank south again. Morty was right.

Plucking around four hundred in twenties out, I thrusted them deeply into my jacket pocket.

'We should get out of here,' I said. 'I've still got a night ahead of me driving. I'll drop you back.'

Snipping the lock on the way out, it occured to me that Jo was not with me. I hadn't felt her around since it happened. Had I done the right thing?

Our steps clopped in the cathedral echo of the stairwell. Looking behind me, I looked for Jo but she had gone. As if swallowed up.

We hit the bottom, passed through to the ground floor corridors and walked along the chessboard linoleum.

'What about our deal?' said Morty.

'What do you mean?'

'My little darling. You know my habits.'

'I thought we had tomorrow sorted out for that?'

'I'm hungry now, Bill.'

'She'll be at work probably. Can't you wait?'

'I'll tell you what. Let's find out for ourselves.'

Morty stopped sharply at Jasmines front door and rapped his knuckles on it. It opened quickly.

'Hello, baby,' Morty said.

'Hey, lover,' said Jasmine.

Jasmine was dressed to kill. The same short black number, I saw her in that first night. Hugging her hips, keeping her secrets. Her hair was teased in just the same careless way. But she was different. There was lucidity in her grey-blue eyes. There was intention.

It had opened my eyes for the first time. Virgin rebirth.

'Come on, Bill,' Morty said, 'coming in or what?'

'I've got to get back. There are people waiting on me.'

'Oh but I insist, Bill,' Morty said planting his palm into the small of my back and guiding me in. 'There's all sorts of things we have to discuss – to get off our chests.'

'I haven't got the time.'

'We'll make time, Bill,' Morty said and shoved me through to fall onto the disarrayed floor.

'He's a dark horse, our Bill,' Morty said. 'Got rid of Alan without me.'

'I told you. He had some sort of seizure. A coronary.'

'Shut up,' said Jasmine. She lands a kick full in my groin.

Electric fire. Bruising aftermath. Deep sob.

'But you didn't do anything for him,' Morty said as if nothing had occurred. 'You came to see me. No hospital. No CPR. Did you check out what you did to his face? That makes you culpable, Bill. A bad man. I'm almost envious of you. To watch him go like that – it must have been grand...sublime.'

I didn't answer. Maybe defiance, maybe guilt. It was all too recent. I didn't know anymore.

Morty stooped down and punched me full in the face. The cartilage in my nose popped.

Tears brimmed. Red-hot iron. Mouth breaths.

'Kill him, Benny,' Jasmine gloated.

'Shut up...But then you had to turn on me,' Morty said. 'Thought you could seduce my girl. Save her. And then what were you planning, Bill?'

What was there to say? Empty nothings.

'He cried like a baby, Benny,' Jasmine said. 'Wanted his mummy.'

'I told you to shut up,' Morty said calmly. He struck Jasmine across the cheek open-handed. She bore it and slapped him back. Morty's face cracked like a whip.

He smiled. 'That's my girl.' Then he kicked me full in the stomach.

One desperate gulp. No air. Bowels quivered.

'See Bill, my baby likes it rough. So do I. Which is good for both of us. Give and take. Not a flowers and candy sort of a lass, you might say.'

A kick caught my ribs. It was all one kind of pain now. Dull hurt.

'I do like you, Bill. You're my kind of guy. School of hard knocks – that blue collar honesty. So I'll take your keys and we'll be off. With Brian's little bag of course.' He wrapped an arm around Jasmine. 'The little woman and I are planning a trip. Sydney...who knows? May even start a brood.' He kissed her on her red cheek. 'You'd like that, wouldn't you honey?'

He was not waiting for an answer. Another kick and I felt nothing and started to crawl away. Fingers scrambled in the pile and hit steel.

'Give them up to me, Bill. Don't want her digging around in your pockets. She can get a tad feisty.'

My other hand pulled the keys clear and dropped them beside me. Morty stepped to pick them up. I rolled and plunged the scissors hard into the top of his shoe. Tongue central.

He dropped and screamed. One long howl.

As I rose, I cracked Jasmine low on the jaw. My hips rolled all my weight behind it. She dropped cold on the ground. Motionless. King hit.

In moments, I was at the door running, trying to ignore my basketball groin and my shard of a nose. The door became larger and I was through.

The howls continued. Fucking wimp.

Out at the car I realised that the keys still lay next to Morty. He might be a wimp but so was I. I wasn't venturing back into that. Opening the passenger door, I grabbed the white plastic bag, pulled it clear and hobbled towards Karangahape Road.

Back to the dark.

24.

I stumbled adrift. Great North Road ended and city central proper began. To the left of me, the smell of money permeated my stinging nose. Ponsonby, 12.00 a.m. Fancy cars, designer clothes and chic urbanites congregated just out of sight. Straight ahead it was more mundane, hints of seedy undertones, secret liaisons and veiled peril. On the corner of Ponsonby and Karangahape Roads, I stumbled into the gas station with the lone attendant. He sat behind a Plexiglas shield, ventilated with small holes from which he could speak and breathe. Behind him sat his goods, overpriced and stale.

'Are you alright, sir?' he said to me. His voice was baffled by the barrier. 'You don't look so good.'

'I need some water. A couple of bottles.'

'Certainly sir, what sort would you like?'

'I don't care. It's not for drinking.'

'Well that's all very well, but how will I know what to get? There are many brands to choose.'

My head pounded. My temper broke and spilled forth. 'Just bring me the cheapest kind you have. I don't fucking care.'

He looked back at me, a look of superiority in his expression. It said, he was the one in charge here. Not me. 'No need for that, sir,' he said, a quiet reproach in his tone. 'I have what you need. What size: 750ml or a litre?'

I didn't care. 'Two litre bottles.' I replied. My annoyance stayed in check.

'That'll be six dollars eighty.'

'For water?'

'Six dollars eighty.'

I reached into the plastic bag, foraged around and pulled out a crumpled twenty. I placed it in the security compartment and wiped the blood still dripping from my nose with a sleeve.

The attendant's hand slid the shutter closed with a metallic crash, he withdrew to the rear of the station beyond my sight and returned with two clear bottles. He rung my money into the till, pulled out the change – ten dollars and some gold – and crammed it all into his side of the tray. Metallic clang and it was at my end once more.

Water and money. How much more did a victim need?

'Thank you, sir. Have a nice night.'

'Does it look like I'm having a good time,' I snarled, kicking the wall in front of me to back my point.

The attendant stepped back, even though he is protected by inch thick plastic. 'If you cause any trouble I'll call the cops,' he said. 'They'll be here in seconds.'

Waving him off, I retreated to the dark recesses of the forecourt boundary and sat on a kerb. Screwing one of the plastic bottles open, I poured it gingerly over my face. It stung like acid. My eyes watered once more. Slow relief.

I threw a little in my mouth, sluiced it round and spat it down on the asphalt before me. My gums were ravaged, the inside of my lips were swollen and tender.

I was thirty-eight years old.

Reaching for a cigarette, I realised that they were damaged beyond repair. I needed some more. The attendant peered at me in the gloom. Shit.

The walk that took me back to him was laced in regret.

'I need some cigarettes,' I said sweetly.

'Are you sure you want to get them from me?' he said.

'Yes.'

'What sort were you after, sir?'

'Rothmans – twenty pack.'

Throwing the change just given to me back into the receptacle, I pondered the usefulness of simple politeness. Thinking of Morty, I knew the danger of it. The blue and white pack came back through the other side with what was left of my original twenty. I grabbed the packet.

'Keep the change,' I said. 'For the trouble.'

'You're too kind sir,' he said, sniffing at the one gold and minimal silver coinage in front of him. 'But it is against company policy. I could lose my job.'

'Suit yourself.'

Wandering back to my kerbside position, I discovered my precious water has disappeared into the night. Only a small puddle of spit remains of it. Who would steal what was freely available in taps. The house of Auckland was a cruel place.

Sitting down I pulled the cellophane wrappings off, opened and removed the silver foil from the top, extracted the product, placed it firmly between bruised lips and lit up. The taste of tobacco did not ease me.

Nothing belonging to this place eased me anymore.

Sore knees and cracked ribs propelled me upwards and I stood once more alone in the world. There would be taxis further down Karangahape Road. That is, if one would deign to drive someone in such a sorry state. My legs stumbled forwards. Once again, each step jarred every wound.

Up and down the street, people cruised in small bands. They made small envelopes of noises that came to me frivolous and far too happy. Didn't they know what happened around them? The ugliness.

Onwards I travelled, people skirted me in small circles. I imagined how I appeared to them. Bloodied, scarred, a battlefield of malice. I must have suddenly appeared to them out of the dark like a fictional creature. Far too grotesque too be possibly real.

Crossing a side street, I glanced at a figure bent in the window of a parked car, its motor still running. After seconds, the figure opened her side of the car up and clambered inside. The vehicle sputters off, turned a corner and disappeared.

'Looking for any business tonight?'

The voice that crept up from behind is husky and low. I turned around to see, wrapped up in pseudo-fur, micro skirt and tights, a woman. I think.

'No,' I said, 'I need to get a taxi.'

'I could suck you off real cheap. I usually work in a car but it's so quiet tonight. No customers.'

'No,' I reaffirmed, 'Maybe some other time.' I wandered away, leaving her on her corner.

I made it to the overbridge. It was busier here: more light, more bands of people clustered together in little tribes and sounds from cars, bars and city life.

Breathless after little bursts of exercise, I sat myself on a bus stop seat and watched the traffic go by.

I didn't want to know what was different about this place now. That something that still eluded me had become so unimportant in the greater scheme of things, that I wondered why the question ever came up. It was just different. I was different and I hadn't the energy to wonder anymore.

I wished I still had a bottle of water. It would wash the stink of the cars from me.

'I'm a man of the streets, you know,' a voice rose beside me, 'Gotta cigarette brother?'

Smiling, despite myself, I turned to Mr Dreadlocks parked up beside me on the red-painted bench. 'Is that right?' I said. 'I guess you deserve to be.'

'Of course I deserve to be,' he said. 'I've been here the longest. It's mine.'

I threw him my packet and lighter. 'Keep it.' I said. 'A king needs a few cigarettes on him at all times.'

'How about two bucks?'

Steerforth's cash weighed my jacket pocket down. Snatching the twenties that sat inside the envelope of fabric, I thrust it into his hands. 'A king needs a stash as well.'

I didn't need it anymore.

'You scabby old prick,' a voice came from the other side. Of course it was there. 'I leave you for five minutes and you're a rich man.' She followed it up with a cackle: street sore.

'I'm gonna get laid tonight,' he said.

'Not from me, you ugly old bastard,' she said.

'Who're you calling ugly?'

'You. Give us some.'

'Fuck off.'

Leaving them there I felt alleviated for the moment. At least someone won. It would have been a shame if no one did. Would he be a king in a new millennium?

Standing, I drifted further upwards. Their voices garbled and lost meaning. My heart darkened the further I stepped away.

People didn't look at you in the city. They may look where you were walking, the body you inhabited. But their gazes only hit you at surface level. It took an engagement of the eyes to understand someone. Here they looked everywhere but there. To do otherwise meant caring. And no one seemed to care here.

Finding a taxi just past Leo O'Malley corner, I pulled open the passenger door and fitted myself inside.

'Where to, mister?' said my driver: Middle Eastern descent probably, with a thick accent and a penchant for a raga beat being played over his radio.

'Where indeed? Sandringham Road. You know *Nymphs*?' I tried to instil joviality in my timbre. Put him at ease about my battered appearance.

'I do. Looking for a good night out?' he said, throwing the car into gear and turning out with no apparent concern for the night traffic.

'Just trying to get through it.'

The beat was fused with a keening wail of a vocal that I had no understanding of. The music whirled like a hurdy-gurdy around the car. It filled the dead air around me, relaxed me into my seat and lulled me into a sense of comfort. I reached into the plastic bag and peeled him a twenty.

'Will that get me there?' I asked.

'I don't know, sir' he said.

I reached back and gave him another. 'Keep the change.'

He smiled, a murmur of glint in his eyes. 'Thank you, sir.' Pulling a card from his visor, he handed it to me and continued: 'Ring me on this number after. I'll give you a good rate.'

I did not have the heart to tell him that this was the last ride I'd take off anyone else again. Wasn't his problem. Accepting the card, I pocketed it, sat back and closed my eyes.

I couldn't find her in here.

Normally I only had to think of her and she came to me. Now there was only a void. There was only me, a taxi driver and a car on a road.

Nothing else.

The journey did not take so long. Once past Symonds Street, the traffic dropped away to a trickle. I was sick of looking at the road. Let it think about me for a change. Closing my eyes, I let sleep take me. Alone for the first time in years.

***

He shook me conscious. We were parked opposite *Nymphs,* her winking sign still glowed azure.

It did not invite me.

Grabbing the bag that rested now at my feet, I opened my side of the car.

'Thanks mate.'

'No, thank you sir. Call me later and I'll come right away.'

It was a heartfelt groan that exited me from the taxi. As it sped off, back towards the city, I wondered how much cash he grabbed while I was asleep. Enough to make it worth his while, I hoped.

'Good on you, pal,' I said to the retreating tail lights.

I crossed the wide silent road, empty of everything except streetlights and crossed down the alley. I looked at the graffiti that adorned the weatherboard wall once more. It still meant nothing to me, but now it seemed to speak volumes. It came as a tribal chant, telling the story of this place, in the manner of the ancient ones. Whoever they might be.

At the end, beside my car, the Harley sat low and evil against the homely lines of my Toyota. Its engine still tinkled in the cold, rebelling against it. Tama can't have been here long.

I would be here even less.

Reaching once more inside the plastic, I take good handfuls of cash and stuffed both pockets. Creeping to the bike – for what practical reason, I didn't know – I placed the bag on the jail-bar handles. The bag crinkled in the slight breeze and billowed for a bit. A single twenty escaped and fluttered skywards. I studied its flight and hoped it found a home.

'Are you leaving without me?' her voice said.

I turned and even though it is night she is bathed in eternal sunlight. 'There's one more thing to do and you don't want to be there for that.'

'Back to your wife?'

I closed my eyes. 'No. She left me. It's all over.'

'Take me with you.'

'Maybe in the next life.'

With nothing left to see, I opened my car and sat inside, ignoring the need for a cigarette and fitted the key into its home. For the first time in living memory, the engine fired at the first turn. The engine did not groan at the effort, putting on a brave face.

Unlike its driver.

It ignored my thoughts as it pulled out into Sandringham Road heading in a general southerly direction. Put aside my years of condemnation, and my criticism and drove like its proud European counterpart. Full steam ahead.

***

Cars blended with road. Mixed with night as I turned onto the Great South Road. Once an important street, now reduced to the rank of a poor substitute by arterials and solid veins of the motorways. I drove down its deserted flanks, unconcerned with its tragic destiny. It was just a road, after all.

A poorly lit sign told me a motel with vacancies was approaching. Pulling into the car park, I turned off the ignition, groaned again as I forced myself out the driver's seat, hobbled to a manager's office with the light turned off. The buzzer rang loud in the quiet of dusk, a light turned on after a time and the door was answered.

'Do you know what time it is?'

'No. Pretty late I guess. I need a room.'

'Are you alone?'

'Always.'

He named a price and I handed over some twenties, crumpled and greasy. I declined his offer to show me the room, accepted the key with the bright plastic number tag and trudged to my unit. As I turned over the key in the lock, I realised I couldn't remember what the manager looked like.

Falling on top of the covers, I closed my eyes and thought of a woman in soft focus, hanging on a wall in lurid colour, watching over me from afar.

25.

My eyes felt swollen. I opened them to the daylight arching in past the gauzed netting curtains of the bedroom window. With no healthy sinuses with which to breathe through, my tongue had become furry and the back of my throat bloodied and sharp through the night. Rolling slowly off the bed, I traipsed to the bathroom, gingerly pushed my face under the tap and let the water that flowed cascade over my face. Closing my eyes to the sting, I opened my mouth, filled it with the cool liquid and tipped my head back.

I gargled and spat.

The residue in the basin was red and frothy as it dawdled anti-clockwise down the plughole. A slight stain was left around the rim of the drain.

I slowly peeled the suit off my tired frame and turned the shower on at a lukewarm temperature, not too cold to shock. I stepped inside and let the gentle cascade take me from my broken head to my better off toes.

Where had she gone? It was empty here in the cubicle, the steam slowly rising from my shoulders on what appeared to be a too bright winter's morning. I forgot what day it was now – the weekend maybe. Since Steerforth slowly had turned blue in the passenger seat, she had been missing. I did what she wanted and how had she repaid me? Taken Dominic and disappeared for ever from my life.

From my life.

I switched the handle briefly too cold to shock me further awake and I stepped out onto chilly linoleum. Frigid cool. The towel blanketed me as I carefully dried and wrapped myself into it. Looking in the mirror, I studied what gazed back at me. Symmetry was no longer an issue with my face. It wasn't as bad as it felt. Although my nose is swollen and misshapen, my eyes have only slight dark rings around them, which gave me a look of a tragic clown. Appropriate really, for I wasn't anything else now.

A sharp rap on the outside door broke me from my reverie. I pulled the towel tighter around my waist and limped to the door, each step an exercise in breathing. I opened it cautiously at first.

'11 o'clock clear out,' the manager said. 'It's 10.30 now...'

The manager was younger than I had thought last night. He had the look of an up and coming professional waiting to break into the big time. Maximum profits and minimal overheads. What the hell was he doing choosing this type of venture? This way meant a slow draining of the soul. It showed in the fret etched lines of his face.

'Can I pay for another night? I'll be gone by then.'

The manager's face eased somewhat. A tension was released and a business-like smile transformed his features. 'Certainly.'

'Wait there,' I said and stomped back to the suit that lay abandoned on the bathroom floor. Pulling the money from the jacket pocket and more from the trousers, I fanned it out on the patterned linoleum. Extracting six twenties I returned and handed it to him. 'Is that enough?'

'More than enough, sir. Is there anything I can get for you?'

'You can tell me where the nearest liquor shop is.'

'You haven't been here before. It's over the road.'

I followed the line of his finger over the highway. It is an old style pub, unpretentious and low sitting – the kind where public bars still exist. In front a small car park sat with an unobtrusive bottle-shop behind.

'You should find what you're looking after,' he said. 'I don't want any noise though.'

'I'll be like a church mouse,' I said.

The door shut in his face like a trap. My suitcase still held two unused shirts that were still cellophane housed. Taking the red one out and laying it on the bed, I returned to the bathroom and picked my suit off the floor. I kicked the strewn money, spreading it into disorder on the carpet.

The suit had also fared better than I thought. The benefit of a basic black – hid the shit well.

Giving it a cursory brush over, I stepped back into the trousers, placed the shirt over top of my cracked ribcage and pulled the jacket around me.

The Italian shoes had not made it through untouched. Scuff marks marred the hand tooled leather, making them appear battered and war torn. I didn't bother with socks just jimmied them over my bare feet. Grabbing a couple of twenties from the floor, I exited and greeted the morning.

I hadn't seen the sun for an age. Spreading my arms wide – trying not to wince – I looked skyward and enjoyed the morning's warmth.

The tops of my toes and the backs of my heels blistered almost immediately as I hobbled over the Great South Road. Entering the bottle store, I sought the shelves for the good stuff. Swedish vodka not the tripe they fobbed off as Russian. Making my purchase, I entered the day again and stumbled back.

***

Inside my room, I took a grubby glass from the cupboard and poured two fingers of vodka and top it with tonic. I drunk it down fast and repeated the process. This time pouring a stronger mix. It did not take long to polish half a bottle.

Not drunk but brave, I picked out my only tie and laid it out on the unmade sheets. Back at the kitchen, I downed another quick two mixers.

The problem with choosing a cliché way to go was that is never as simple as it seemed. Take me for instance. My first choice would have been pills. It seemed peaceful. Just down a bottle with a few drinks and lay down to sleep. What they didn't tell you though, is that there was a twofold problem in choosing to go this way. Firstly, actually getting access to something that would actually do the job was problematic. A good barbiturate was hard to get prescribed these days. Doctors would rather give you something to keep you up and active amid your shitty life. Mother's Little Helpers, in the old forms, weren't in vogue anymore.

Secondly, you had the luxury of changing your mind halfway through. You could have a light bulb moment and rush to the bathroom, stick your fingers down your throat, tickle your tonsils a little and you're out again.

Fuck that. If you were going to do a job – as my drunken old man used to yell at me – do it bloody properly. Choose a method where there is no going back and stick with it. And make sure you attend to the little things. It made the large job run that much more smoothly.

The method I had chosen also had challenges attached to it. That's why I spent time researching it. The problem with hanging yourself was finding somewhere private to do it and finding somewhere to do it from. The tried and true method was from a tree. And sure, there were plenty of secluded trees in the world from which you could carry out the act. But when I went I wanted to prepare my body for its eventual discovery. Leave symbols to let them know why.

Showy I know, but it all had to mean something – didn't it?

Finding somewhere inside to do it also had its trials. The modern building did not usually have low slung rafters. Light sockets and ceiling hooks didn't really have the stress tolerances to bear the weight of an adult male. Even for a weasel faced emaciated specimen like myself.

So what did the earnest tradesman do when presented with a practical problem like this? He researched it and found a reasonable and efficient way to get through it. And that's what I did.

Motels came with a wardrobe in every bedroom. With a strong metal bar from which to hang your clothes. I didn't have a suitable belt but I did have the tie I was married in. It all seemed perfect. Everything I could have possibly needed was at hand.

I poured another drink in the kitchen and swallowed it fast. It did not taste so fine. The bite of the tonic twisted and crawled in my guts. Expensive vodka made you just as sick.

My photos were in my pocket – all that was left of my life. Reliable memories. I fanned them around the entrance way. From the bathroom, I collected up the cash and arranged it around the photos. Dominic's picture sat at the apex. My crowning glory.

The effect reminded me of the corona of a morning sun.

I had to pick my steps through the display, to cinch the tie at an appropriate length from the bar and I carried in a footstool from the kitchen. A good tradesman would have done this first. But I got there in the end. My altar was ready for the master of ceremonies to perform his duties.

I stepped up on the footstool. Slipped my head into the noose.

I left no notes to let them know why. The photographs should explain everything to anyone that could be bothered to find out. If anyone existed like that. Maybe a coroner.

Well this was it, girl. I was coming to you again – and the boy. I cinched the noose tight behind my jaw line, ensuring that the carotid would cut off blood to the brain. I had read that it made for a more pleasant death.

I stepped off.

I didn't want to die.

Darkness.

She was not here. No one was.

I crashed to the floor.

Life was not as simple as it was in books.

***

I came to on the floor. Fucking typical. Story of my life.

It took only a cursory look to tell that the bar was strong enough but the wooden supports that held it in place were not. Never rely on someone else's work. I lay on the bed and closed my eyes.

It had been a long day.

Evening had already arrived when I awoke. My head pounded but I welcomed it. It told me that I was alive. And for the first time in a long time I was glad about the fact.

She was never going to be there. I jumped off and saw nothing. No shining bright lights guiding me to heaven. There had been nothing at all. This revelation was like being reborn.

Jo and Dominic were gone and no matter what I did, I would never get back to them.

'You really are a stupid man,' she said.

She was there at the door. 'How did you get in?'

'You ask that but don't wonder how I escape from a painting? I think you're a little delusional.'

'You just might be right.'

I scooped up the money and put it back into my pockets. Everything else I left behind me when I closed the door. I didn't need it anymore.

Jumping back into the Toyota, I headed back to the motorway on-ramp and headed south.

***

My painted lady filled my mind as I headed past Papakura and beyond. She smiled at me from her Pacific landscape. A warm genuine smile, wanting nothing other than to now that I was here. In the background, a lone gull wheeled and careered on a lurid skyline, playing forever in an eternal updraft.

'Where will we go now?'

I looked over at her barely clothed body, her hair still swept by an unseen breeze. 'Where would you like?' I said.

'I want to see the ocean...the real ocean. I want to smell the salt. Feel sand beneath my toes.'

'I have a friend in Golden Bay with a house. Maybe we could stay there awhile. We could see the whales...' I turned back to the road and watched the white painted centre line guide my way. 'You'll probably get sick of me though. Just like her.'

She whispered softly in my ear, 'As long as I can see the ocean and you keep me free, I'm yours forever.' Her scent was a deep scarlet orchid: wild and exotic. 'You have always been mine.'

'We'll see,' I said.

As I headed through the centre of the Bombay Hill's cleavage, my rear view mirror showed me Auckland. The Sky Tower glowed magenta and green, looking proud and phallic, surrounded by a halo of streetlight. Oranges, whites and cold purples clashed and mingled in the palette. Auckland was a multitude of garish colour painted on a soft black canvas. It looked busy, moving headlights barely visible in the melange and illusory as nothing very real ever happened there.

Moving towards the dawn of a new age, it still looked the same.

It looked velvet dark.

ABOUT THE AUTHOR

Brent Partner is a writer, academic librarian, husband and father.

He has a BA (Hons) degree in English and was one of only eight University of Auckland graduates accepted into the inaugural *Writing the Novel* course convened by Witi Ihimaera and Stephanie Johnson in 2004.

Brent has a passion for crime, science fiction and fantasy fiction and writes across these genres.

You can find him at: http://brentpartner.com

Sign up for his newsletter and receive a free short story

Printed in Great Britain
by Amazon